I0580695

Loki:

A Paranormal Protector Tale

Book 2 in the Heart of Ice series

DEMELZA CARLTON

ONE

It was a perfect night for fishing. Loki barely had to drop his hook in the water before another cod took the bait, ready to be hauled into his boat before he dropped his hook again. Another hour, and he'd have managed to catch enough fish to last them until next month.

Until the fish stopped biting.

After perhaps a quarter hour without so much as a nibble, Loki pulled up his line. The bait was still there, but the fish must have gone. He eyed the baskets of fish he'd already caught. He could go home now, with his bumper catch, or he could head out into deeper water, and see if he could find the fish again.

Then again, if something had scared them, he might sail off the edge of the world and still not find them. Or worse, if there was a sea monster about, it might decide he'd make a tastier meal than any fish…

Speaking of meals, it was likely dinner time, and Mother would have his waiting. Best he head home. He could go fishing again tomorrow.

Decision made, Loki turned his boat toward the shore.

Only to see a crowd gathered there, a great number of shadows on the sand. As he watched, new figures joined the throng…but not from the village. No, they walked out of the water, like nykr. An army of nykr, headed for the village.

Loki forgot about the fish, and his boat. Much like the nykr, he, too, could transform, and he took the swiftest form he knew, flying as a falcon back to the village.

"The nykr are coming!" he cried as he burst into the longhouse.

Mother and Father exchanged a telling glance.

Mother shook her head. "Nykr never attack the land. Not unless they are under a spell..." She paled.

"This Jarl Erik's doing. Him and his witch," Father spat. "How many did you see, boy?"

Loki swallowed. He hadn't stopped to count. "At least a hundred. More, maybe."

Another glance passed between his parents, before his father nodded.

"Run, boy, run, to warn Odin!" Mother said, even as she and his father reached for their spears.

Loki looked longingly at the stack of spears, wanting to fight, too.

"Bring back help. Warn them, so they can

come and fight off Erik's raiders before they reach anyone else!" Mother hissed. "No one can run faster than you!"

That was true, Loki had to admit. No one else could shift their form into any animal they wished, like he could.

So he shifted back into a gyrfalcon, and flew.

Flew…but not fast enough.

He could scarcely breathe by the time he'd reached Odin, tired enough so that he almost tumbled out of the sky at the man's door. Then he'd had to remember how to shift back to human, so he could wake Odin, and tell him what had happened.

Precious moments flew by until Odin and his warriors were ready.

Loki flew ahead, leading them onward…to what was left of his home.

When Odin's men arrived, they found him back in his human form, crouched beside the body of what he barely recognised as his mother. The village was a smoking ruin, and he hadn't managed to find his father's body. Maybe he was in one of the still burning houses, or worse, burned to ash already.

There was no sign of the nykr, except for the carnage they'd left behind.

Tears and snot had streamed down his face, like the orphaned child he was, but Odin had ordered him to rise, and Loki had, unable to disobey.

Then a spear was placed in his hand, a spear taller than he was, and as Loki's fist clenched around it, he swore he would make Erik and his men pay. Erik had stolen his family from him, and Loki would spend every breath in his body making sure Erik knew the same pain.

Whatever it took.

TWO

"Can we get party pies? I want party pies!" six year old Jojo cried, grabbing the biggest packet she could find.

"Stick it up your jumper," Mum hissed.

Shocked, she fell silent. Two girls in her class had gotten in BIG TROUBLE for saying that to someone. They'd had to go on a timeout for the rest of recess and they hadn't been allowed to play at all. Jojo couldn't believe Mum would say something so bad.

"Quickly!" Mum said, shoving the packet under her actual…oh.

The icy plastic froze her skin through her thin t-shirt, plastered against her chest and tummy under Jojo's jumper. She began to shiver, and then she started to cry.

Mum jabbed her finger at the floor. "Stay right here, and I'll be back in a minute. Don't move!" She dashed off to the end of the aisle and vanished.

Jojo sat down on the shop floor and bawled, trying to pull the packet out but the ice was now stuck to her sweater and it wouldn't come out, so she cried louder.

Then some woman she didn't know leaned over her. "What's your name, honey?"

Jojo shook her head, clamping her mouth shut. Mum and her teacher had said never to talk to strangers, and she'd never seen this lady before in her life.

A minute later, another stranger appeared – a man this time. When Jojo refused to talk to him either, the two of them marched her into an office with lots of screens on the wall, showing the inside of the supermarket without any colour, like it was a really old movie. Except it wasn't a movie, it was now, because Mum was in one of the aisles, this one full of bottles, and she was sliding two big bottles into her bag, followed by a third.

The man and woman weren't paying attention to the screens, though. Instead, they were trying to pull the packet of pies out from under Jojo's sweater, while she screamed for her mum. Mum had told her to put them there, and Mum's punishments were way worse than a timeout if she didn't do what Mum said.

"What are you doing to my daughter?" Mum demanded, her voice thunderous.

Jojo dashed under the desk, desperate to get away from Mum's fury, hugging the icy plastic to her chest. She'd done what Mum asked. She was a good girl.

The man and woman stumbled over their

words, explaining that they'd found the little girl crying in one of the aisles, and how she wouldn't let go of the pie packet.

Mum glanced at her and shook her head. "She gets meltdowns like this sometimes. There's nothing I can do except take her home and hope she calms down." She seized Jojo's hand. "Come on. We're going home." Her bag clinked, but no one except Jojo seemed to notice.

"But the pies…" the woman began.

The man hushed her. "They're crushed and starting to defrost. Not like we can sell them any more anyway. Besides, it's Christmas Eve. Chalk it up to damaged stock and…let the lady and her daughter take them home. My nephew has meltdowns like that, too, and my sister's a saint with everything she does for that kid. You must be, too, ma'am." He nodded respectfully to Mum.

Mum gave a tight smile. "Thank you. Merry Christmas to you, and your sister," she said, hustling Jojo out of there.

In the carpark, they passed one of the naughty girls from school, skipping as she held her mum's hand. "Don't forget to get cookies for Santa, Mum, or he won't come and bring presents!" she said.

Her mum frowned. "Don't you think Santa's fat enough? I bet he gets cookies from everyone, and he can't eat all of them. No, it's his reindeer who do all the work, pulling his sleigh. We should get snacks for them."

"But what kind of cookies do reindeer eat, Mum?"

Her mum shook her head. "Reindeer don't eat cookies. They eat carrots. So we'll buy a big bag of carrots, so there's enough for everyone."

The girl jumped up and down. "So if they eat all their carrots, they'll grow big and strong, and be able to bring even more presents?"

"Maybe. We'll see," her mum said, as they headed into the shop.

"Come on, Jojo!" Mum insisted, yanking her hand.

Jojo did her best not to anger Mum any more all the way home, and Mum must have seen how good she was, because she cooked her a couple of the party pies before she opened one of the bottles from her bag and started drinking.

There wasn't any tomato sauce, not like there was at school, but Jojo ate the pies anyway, even as they burned her tongue. It was already the best Christmas ever, and it might get even better, if she could get Santa to come and bring presents. If even Mum thought she'd been a good girl, then surely Santa would see it this year.

Much later, when Mum's bottle was almost empty and she'd started snoring on the couch, Jojo crept into the kitchen. She knew Santa usually came down the chimney, and they didn't have a chimney (one of the other reasons Mum said Santa never came to their house), but there was a round hole in the ceiling with a fan in it, gaping big and black and scary, just like a chimney, so Jojo figured that would do.

She dug through the drawer at the bottom of the fridge, between a bag of black leaves that she thought might be lettuce and a bag of white fluffy tomatoes, to where she remembered seeing some carrots. She found the carrot bag right down the bottom, with just one carrot in it. It was kind of soft and wobbly, not like the crunchy carrot sticks they had to eat at school, but it was still mostly orange and it didn't smell bad.

She stuck the carrot on the counter, under the hole in the ceiling, so the reindeer could see and smell it from the roof.

She considered putting it on a plate, but reindeer were animals – they didn't use plates. She knew that because her teacher had said her cat stole a pizza off the bench when she wasn't looking once. Jojo couldn't imagine a cat eating pizza. Did it hold the pizza in its paws, or just lick off the toppings? And what if there was pineapple on it? Ugh.

Shaking her head, Jojo went to bed.

The next morning, her mum was still snoring on the couch, though the bottle was definitely empty now, and Jojo crept into the kitchen to see if Santa had left any presents.

The bench was empty, except for the carrot.

Jojo's shoulders sagged. The reindeer hadn't eaten it.

Which meant the naughty girl and her mum must be wrong. Reindeer didn't like carrots.

Then and there, Jojo swore she'd find out what reindeer did like, and everything else about them, so that one day, she'd know exactly how to catch one, and that would be her new best Christmas ever.

Then someone snored, waking Jorunn up from her dream before it got any darker. Before she'd grown too old to throw tantrums as distractions while Mum shoplifted, and her mother had begun teaching her all she knew about stealing stuff.

Which had been a lot, especially after some idiot in the Centrelink office had decided to try and get Mum off welfare payments by sending her on a training course for shop security guards. Once Mum knew what they were trained to look for, she'd started stealing more than just groceries and alcohol. Stuff she could sell. And she'd made Jorunn do it, too, because kids could get away with way more than adults could, without anyone calling the police.

Even now, when Jorunn walked into a shop, she found herself automatically scanning the space for cameras and security measures, exits and staff. Not that she'd stolen anything in years, and she had no intention of ever doing it again.

Instead, she'd been working her arse off to get all the way to Norway, with a Harald Medal, no less, to fund her research. Talk about a fresh start. No one here knew about Mum, or all the stuff she'd stolen. Here, she wasn't Jojo any more, the kid yoyoing in and out of trouble like her namesake, while Mum drank the proceeds of her thieving and half the time forgot she even had a daughter.

Here, she was Jorunn Gabard, PhD

candidate and reindeer expert, here to see the real thing in the wild.

Another snore. Ah, it was Sibyl, her roommate. If you could call someone you shared both a tent and the Harald Medal with a roommate.

Better than the alternative – Saint Nik, the arsehole from hell.

But she'd take a whole camp full of Niks if it meant getting away from her mother, so she could live her own life, and make her own mark on the world. Because she was a survivor, and she wasn't going to let another selfish arsehole get in her way again.

Sibyl shifted onto her side, and the snoring stopped.

Jorunn couldn't help but smile. Sibyl wasn't an arsehole, at least. Even in her sleep, she was the sweetest, nicest person Jorunn had ever met. She even felt sorry for Nik not getting to go to Egypt, when everyone else muttered about it being karma.

But karma worked both ways – and she was

going to soak up all the good karma now, after the years of hell she'd endured to get here.

She'd find reindeer, whatever it took.

THREE

Loki soared through the sky on silent wings. He'd left Odin's army encamped in the pass, and he'd return to them before dawn, when he was done scouting. Of course, he'd have to shift back into human form first, so as not to shock anyone. Odin knew about his ability to shapeshift, and the other magics he'd inherited from his mother, but no one else — not even Thor — knew the true extent of his abilities.

Enough that the others knew he was a brilliant scout, with a way with animals. Animals knew, recognising him for what he was, but most of them didn't mind. Sleipnir certainly hadn't. Thor's goats, though...those beasts had gone out of their way to make his life difficult. He preferred horses and reindeer, though he was partial to a haunch of roast goat, and he suspected they'd known that.

But tonight's scouting mission wasn't about Thor or even Odin. No, now it was finally time to visit vengeance on Jarl Erik.

Nothing but pristine snow in the pass, and on the plain below. He could hear prey in their burrows beneath the snow, and between the piled boulders that were too sharp to be snowcapped at this altitude, but he didn't stop to hunt. He'd eaten his fill as a human, and he had no intention of remaining a long-eared owl long enough to need to eat in this form.

Odin would make sure there was a big bowl of salt cod pottage waiting for him when he returned with news in the morning.

Now, all he had to do was find Erik's army…

Ah, vermin of a very different kind. The kind that feasted and sang, all unknowing that death was on its way.

There were no nykrs in sight. Only a village with a longhouse larger than the one Odin lived in, filled with men and women making merry.

Not for long, Loki swore as he swooped in.

The thatch roof rustled beneath his talons as Loki settled over one of the largest smoke holes. The vermin within the thatch were nothing to what dwelled beneath it. For in the carved chair at the high table sat a man who could be no one except Jarl Erik, flanked by two men who were surely his sons.

All Loki had to do was sneak into the longhouse and he could end Erik in one stroke. Maybe even his sons, if he was swift enough. Not as an owl, though. Perhaps a lynx…

No. Someone would notice a lynx.

Something smaller, then, which brought death swiftly.

His mother had spoken of such a creature, from the lands far to the south. A snake which could bring death with but one bite. Smaller and less showy than the vipers that rarely killed, but size was no signifier of power when it came to serpents.

A cobra, she'd called it, a snake from the shores of the Caspian Sea, with a hood around its head.

Loki transformed from bird to snake, sensing the fearful fleeing of prey in the thatch as he slithered down to the packed earth floor.

It took him a moment to orient himself in this form, which felt sluggish in the cold night air. All he had to do was bite Erik and he could take wing again, watching Erik's death throes from the safety of the roof.

Loki slithered across the floor, twining up the back of Erik's chair without a soul seeing him.

The best place to bite would be the back of

Erik's neck, for the rest of him was covered in heavy furs. Loki inched his way along the chair back, before venturing up the folds of Erik's cloak. He could almost taste the man's blood, even before he bit him, savouring the saltiness of the evil man's lifeblood.

The man who'd killed his mother, his father, his whole village. Then Thor's parents, kind people who'd taken him in when he had no one. And Sif, young Sif, who might one day have become…

"Father, watch out!"

Someone seized Loki, throwing him to the floor.

He reared up, hissing, at the girl who faced him, as fearless as any warrior. She had the look of Erik, too. His daughter, perhaps? She had called him Father…

"Such a snake is not often seen here, so far from its home," said another female voice.

Loki was lifted into the air, writhing and trying to bite, though no hand touched him this time. No, this was sorcery — magic far more powerful than anything he possessed. The kind of magic that could raise a nykr army...

He found himself face to face with an Eastern woman with dark hair, old enough to be his mother. She squinted at him suspiciously.

"Who would bring such a deadly creature in here?" she mused.

Erik's gaze went to a man seated at the end of the table, holding a squirming girl on his lap as he groped her. "Orm?"

He shoved the girl off his lap and she fled before he could change his mind. "What?"

The Eastern woman flapped her hand. "This is no ordinary snake. In fact, it smells like one of the warriors from across the mountains."

Loki panicked, trying desperately to get away, but all he managed to do was narrowly miss biting his own tail. The witch's magic held him fast. He couldn't even shift into a different shape!

Struggling madly, he was helpless to resist as the witch dropped him into a basket that still smelled strongly of fish, closing the lid over him before he could wriggle out. Her hold on him vanished, but the basket held him as securely as her magic, for no matter how much he bit at the basket, the weave would not release him.

"He is one of Odin's scouts. If he is here, that means Odin is coming. We must prepare for battle," the woman said.

Loki swore, which only came out as an angry hiss, wishing he'd tried to bite the witch before he'd gone for Erik. Or maybe the sharp-eyed daughter, for she was the one who'd caught him. If he ever got out of this basket, he was going to bite them all, every last one, leaving Erik for last, so he could watch all his favourites die before he drew his last breath.

Yes, that would be justice, for all Erik had stolen from him and Odin and Thor and everyone he knew. Erik would die by Loki's hand, or fangs, or whatever he deemed best, but only after he'd lost his family. Loki swore he would not rest until he'd made good on his vow.

FOUR

Jorunn walked her transect with steady, plodding steps, her eyes never leaving the rocks beneath her boots. While she wasn't a stranger to transects and surveys, she was the only person here who'd never worked an archaeological dig before. Her undergraduate degree was in comparative vertebrate biology, and she'd done some research at a deer farm in the south west, before heavy rains had opened up a sinkhole on the property and given her the opportunity to do her honours project on the animal remains in that cave. Instead of going on to a PhD straight away, she'd taken a year to do a graduate diploma in archaeology before applying for this project.

She'd never dared hope to actually win the Harald Medal. In fact, she'd been ready to submit a research proposal for a project at another cave site when the email had come through. But reindeer beat thylacines hands down, at least in her book. One of the other girls on the research team had been as obsessed by extinct megafauna as Jorunn had been by reindeer, and she'd actually accused Jorunn of madness for heading to Norway instead of underground.

But all that time combing caves had sharpened Jorunn's eyesight for artefacts, which gave her an edge in this team. She had the highest find rate among any of them this expedition, with the gap growing every day, Lara told her with considerable satisfaction, when Sibyl was out of earshot.

Poor Sibyl had caught Karl's obsession — she wanted to find an ice man, mummified beneath the ice. Unlike Karl, though, she'd written her research proposal on the likelihood of a Viking village somewhere near the pass — possibly even mythical Utgard from the legends. But while she was looking for dead Vikings, she'd have been better off paying attention to the real, live ones Norway seemed to be full of. Even up here, miles from civilisation, she had three to choose from — Lars, Andreas and Fredrik. Karl was too old and Saint Nik was so far up his own arse Jorunn would be forced to drag Sibyl away and tie her up in the tent if she so much as suggested she might be attracted to him.

Friends did not let friends date arseholes.

Wait, was that…?

A glint of metal caught Jorunn's eye, and she nudged it with her boot. Yep, that was definitely not a rock. Too regular. It looked like a coin or something. She stuck a marker in the ground beside it, held up the GPS and took a photo with her phone.

She straightened, and continued walking.

Three arrows, four coins and several coloured rags later, Jorunn glanced at her watch. Two of the expeditioners had been taken off transects to record the finds, but the rest of them had covered quite a distance, with a couple of hours still to go. "Lars and Andreas, you start recording from here and backtrack until you meet Nik and Sibyl somewhere in the middle. I'm headed up to the ridge to take some pictures of the survey extent so far. Lara and Jorunn…you're on dinner duty, right?"

"Hell no!" Jorunn called back. "We bet on arrowheads and coins, respectively, and I've seen both of them today. Oi, Saint Nik, tell Karl about the coins, will you?"

Nik looked up at the sound of his name, but all he did was stare at her in irritation. Dick.

"Come on Sibyl, you back me up. You saw the coins and arrowheads, didn't you?" Jorunn wheedled.

Sibyl rose from her crouch and came over. "What did you say?"

"I said today was all about coins and arrowheads. I found heaps. How many were there in the end?" Jorunn persisted.

Sibyl shrugged. "I don't know. I didn't see any. I stopped to dig out some of the cloth samples, in the hope we'd find another ancient tunic. I think I found a hood, or a short cloak, and something that might have been a scarf, but I'd want to get them scanned and cleaned up in the lab before we unfold them for a closer look. They looked pretty delicate."

Which meant she'd have to ask Nik, who'd only be even more of an arsehole about it. Ugh.

She gritted her teeth. "Nik, how many coins did we find today?"

He looked blank. "Coins? I haven't seen any coins. Just rags and arrows." He held up the clear collection bag with the day's finds.

Jorunn grabbed it for a closer examination.

There were a few complete arrows – including one with a two-pronged point – but most of the arrowheads were rusted iron or some sort of bone. Each rag got its own bag, to keep the fibres together for later research, in case they fell apart. There wasn't a coin in sight.

Which made no sense. Jorunn dropped the bags back onto the rocks behind Nik and headed back down the slope to the sites she'd photographed with her phone. Sure enough, she had four separate sites with the round discs, and she hadn't seen anything like them in Nik's bags.

The first site she visited was clear – nothing but bare rock, and the little cairn she'd built for her marker was empty. The second site had a lot of loose rock, but no matter how much she pawed through the stones, she couldn't find the coin or whatever it was.

The last two were just as empty. Like she'd imagined the finds, but her phone said otherwise. There'd been something there, and it wasn't there now.

Either something screwy was going on, or someone was stealing stuff.

Jorunn blew out a breath. Or perhaps they had a poltergeist, the spirit of some long dead Viking who was pissed off at Nik for stealing his shirt, who was playing around with them.

Probably for the best that she didn't tell Sibyl, though. Sibyl would either freak out and have nightmares, or insist on a séance in the hope of placating the poor ghost. And maybe asking it a few questions about Viking life here and where the village might be…

Jorunn tucked her phone back in her pocket and trudged back to camp. "Sorry, Lara, looks like you're cooking by yourself tonight, but Sibyl will help you with the dishes, seeing as we haven't found her lost city yet."

And while Lara cooked, Jorunn would take a look through their finds, to see if anything else was missing. Something about this didn't add up.

FIVE

After a night stuck as a snake in that basket, Loki would have killed for a rat to break his fast. Maybe even a mouse. Ah, who was he trying to fool? He'd happily kill Erik and his whole family for nothing, breakfast be damned.

The day dragged on, and Loki dozed sluggishly in his prison, wishing he'd picked any creature instead of a snake. Even a rat would be able to chew its way out of this benighted basket…

Why hadn't he thought of that earlier?

In a blink, Loki the cobra became Loki the rat, though it took somewhat longer for him to chew a big enough hole in the basket to squeeze through. Once out, he abandoned his vermin form altogether, shifting into a stoat. A tiny predator, certainly, but its small size would be an advantage when trying to escape the village, to return to Odin.

"You are a determined fellow, aren't you? First a snake, now a stoat…whatever will you choose to become next? Best not to find out, I think…so a truth spell it shall be!"

Loki swore squeakily as magic enveloped him again, forcing him into a sudden shift back to his own true form. He'd heard of truth spells so powerful they could strip away all illusions, but to feel one working on his own body that he was helpless to resist…

"Damn you, witch. Don't you know Erik is pure evil?" he spat, when he could speak again.

"Evil is rarely pure, and even then, it is surely a matter of perspective. Jarl Erik means to bring magic back into prominence, instead of this silly new religion from the south with its saints and crosses. As the son of a witch yourself, with magic flowing through your veins, surely you see that you are far superior to the spear-wielding warriors in Odin's village? You fight for the wrong side, young shapeshifter. We are your natural allies, not Odin." The witch smiled, a tad too triumphantly for Loki's liking. Almost like she could read his thoughts and liked what she saw.

"Would a natural ally have killed my mother, witch? I will never take up arms against Odin, and with my dying breath, I will oppose Erik, and all who serve him. Especially those who wield evil sorcery in his name." Loki tried to lift a hand to strike the Eastern witch, but he couldn't move. "Release me, foul witch!"

"Erik would not be fool enough to kill a

witch. He is particularly fond of our kind," the witch said.

"Tell that to his nykr army, walking out of the water to slaughter everyone in my village!"

"Ahhh." The witch nodded, understanding. "That was Orm's men you saw. Not nykr at all, though I suppose you would not know the difference between water walkers and ensorcelled stone protectors. Orm's brother's army, cut down when they dared to attack Jarl Erik's village, and given new life as gargoyles, forever bound to serve. The same fate awaits Odin's men, when they come. Pledge your loyalty to Erik, and he may even let you lead them into battle, when the time comes."

Loki hadn't liked Orm before he knew he was a traitor; he liked him even less now. As for the witch…she didn't know him at all.

"I'm no traitor, and I'm no leader, either. You should make this offer to Thor, and see what he says. Big bloke with a hammer. You can't miss him." Thor might like to lead armies, but the slightest hint that he might turn traitor against Odin, a leader who'd been like an older brother to them both, would have him lifting his hammer to smite the witch where she stood. He'd likely succeed, too, with his hammer having the peculiar ability to resist all kinds of magic. Loki had once tried casting an illusion over it to make it look like a fish as a prank, and the bloody thing had just sat there, unchanged.

So he'd enchanted Thor's belt to turn into an eel instead, but only when he fastened the buckle.

Loki had laughed himself sick as Thor tried to free himself of his wiggling belt, before Thor had smacked him in the face with the eel, a blow so hard it split his lip. The blood had been enough to break the spell, but neither of them had noticed as they'd wrestled for quite a while until Odin had ordered them to stop.

Yes, Thor had always beaten him in a fight, but the fighting had been fun. Loki had to find a way to get back to Odin and Thor to warn them about Erik, his witch and the unholy army who knew they were coming.

"Perhaps I will. Fenrir!" the witch barked.

A boy around the same age as Loki entered the longhouse, bowing and ducking his head in deference to the witch. "Yes, Mistress Kun?"

"Our guest tells me Odin travels with a warrior of some renown. Goes by the name of Thor, and he carries a hammer. Do you think you can bring him to me alive during the battle?"

The boy didn't hesitate. "Yes, Mistress Kun."

"What are you doing now?" the witch demanded.

"Bringing these to Miss Astrid, mistress," Fenrir said, brandishing a bunch of bell-shaped flowers.

"Put them in some water. They can wait. I want you to watch our guest, and make sure he stays here for the feast."

"Yes, Mistress Kun."

Leaving him in the charge of a gangly thrall, who wouldn't last a moment in a fight against

Thor. Even Loki was more than a match for him.

Unfortunately, the witch wasn't entirely stupid. "You, shapeshifter. Don't think you can try anything. My truth spell is still upon you. You shall not change form or leave this hall without permission from me or Jarl Erik, or I'll kill your Thor with a snap of my fingers before the battle begins. Your word, or the warrior dies. Do I have it?"

Loki tried to lie, but the words just wouldn't come out. He sighed. "Fine, witch, you have my word."

Now he just had to somehow trick the witch or Erik into sending him out of the longhouse, and he'd be free.

The witch nodded and left, leaving him alone with the boy.

Loki managed a smile. "So, boy, who's Miss Astrid?"

The boy swallowed. "Jarl Erik's and Mistress Kun's daughter. She's our herbwife, and Mistress Kun is training her to be a witch."

"Far too highborn for the likes of you, then," Loki said.

The boy ducked his head and nodded. "But Miss Astrid is kind, and asks me to assist her, bringing her herbs and such." He gestured at the jug holding the flowers.

The girl who'd picked up a venomous snake to save her father. Kind and brave indeed. It was almost a pity she was Erik's daughter, for that meant Loki would have to kill her. Unless there was another way…

"Is she trying to poison someone, then?" Loki asked.

The boy blinked. "No, Miss Astrid would never do that! She's the most marvellous healer. Even better than Mistress Kun." He sounded proud. "She did not ask for the flowers. I…I picked them myself, as a gift. The purple thimbles are her favourite, and they've just started to bloom."

Loki nodded. The boy was clearly smitten with the jarl's daughter. "My mother called them foxgloves."

The boy bobbed his head. "That's what Miss Astrid calls them, too."

"Do you think she'll carry a bunch of them to her wedding, when she's handfasted to Orm?" Loki asked.

The boy's face paled. "She's to marry him?"

Loki shrugged. "It's the only way Erik would keep a man like that loyal, to bind him into his family. It's what I would do." If he was a leader of men who wanted to ensure their loyalty, which of course he wasn't.

The boy's brows furrowed. "But she can't marry Orm. She won't. He's…he's cruel. She's had to heal so many of the serving girls when Orm comes to visit. She knows what he's like, better than anyone. She'll never agree to it."

"What would Jarl Erik do to his daughter if she refused to marry the man her father had chosen for her? A man he needed to make an alliance with?" Loki mused, plucking one of the flowers from the jug and crushing it in his fist.

The boy shivered. "Nothing good. We all have to obey Jarl Erik."

"Maybe you should save the girl. Run away with her, so she doesn't have to marry Orm."

The boy shook his head violently. "Oh, no, Miss Astrid would never do that! She loves her father. Why, only yesterday, she saved him from a strange snake…so brave, picking it up in her bare hands! I could never, not even for Jarl Erik."

"Maybe you should carry her off, then. Slip something into her wine so she falls asleep, and carry her off somewhere far away, where her father will never find her," Loki suggested, plucking another flower before crushing it.

"Oh, no, that would never work. She's the witch's apprentice, and Mistress Kun would find her. She's a powerful enchantress, you see. She can travel anywhere, instantly."

Loki selected a third flower and crushed it, too. "Well, if you want to save Miss Astrid, you'll have to think of something, or her father will give her to Orm."

The boy eyed him thoughtfully. "It would have to be after the battle. We'd have to act swiftly, before Jarl Erik or Mistress Kun could do anything to stop us. Maybe…"

Loki just nodded. There was more than one way for Erik to lose his family, and if some lovesick boy carried his daughter off, that was one less death he'd need to worry about. Call him soft, but he didn't have the stomach for killing women. Oh, he might be able to knock a shieldmaiden unconscious if she attacked him and it was her life or his, but he'd still regret the blow. But if needs must…

"You might want to give her jusquiasmus, not foxglove, though, if you want her to sleep," Loki said.

"Jusquiasmus?" The boy looked blank.

What else had Loki's mother called it? "Henbane. Stinking nightshade?"

The boy's eyes widened. "The stuff the berserkers drink before battle?"

Loki nodded. "That's the one. If you bring me some, I can show you how to prepare it so it just puts her to sleep, instead of turning her into a berserker." And then he'd have two poisons he could use to help him get out of here and back to Odin.

SIX

Jorunn went through all the artefacts twice, just to make sure, but the result was the same. On the days she'd photographed stuff that wasn't in the storage boxes, Nik had been assigned to cataloguing things.

Sometimes Sibyl or Karl had helped out on those days, too, so there'd been three sets of handwriting, but never one of the other guys. Lara helped out sometimes with the transects, but she preferred to leave the actually archaeology stuff to the diggers, as she called them.

So far, Jorunn had managed to avoid cataloguing duty – swapping with Sibyl as often as she could, because Sibyl actually liked that stuff – but maybe tomorrow she should take her turn. Because she couldn't just go to Karl with her suspicions. He'd worked with Nik way longer than he'd worked with her, and probably trusted him, too.

She'd have to actually witness him stealing stuff, and even that might not be enough. She'd watched her thieving mother blatantly deny everything even when she knew she'd stuffed Jorunn's bag or pockets or jumper with stuff she wanted to steal.

God. Having to work alongside Nik all day tomorrow. Kill her now.

"Hey, Lara, can I take a bottle of aquavit to share with Sibyl tonight? That other one I put in my pack's empty," Jorunn said.

"As long as you have a drink for me, and a

toast to my health, grab one whenever you like. Karl's on some sort of health kick, refusing to drink until he finds his ice mummy, and the other men are drinking that horrible German herbal stuff." She shuddered. "At least you Aussie girls have good taste."

Jorunn tipped an imaginary hat to Lara. "We will drink your health with every cup, I promise you. We'd all starve without your wonderful cooking, and the whole expedition would fall apart without you to organise us every day!"

Lara shook her finger warningly. "Don't tempt fate. At this altitude the old Norse gods could still hear you, and take notice. The last thing we want is Loki messing with our expedition. An unseasonal blizzard, a supply run that runs late, or any number of things could go wrong, and even I can't control chaos. If you want my advice, you offer a cup of aquavit to the Norse gods, for the good of this expedition. They like a good drink as much as the rest of us."

Jorunn promised to do that, too. Though she had to admit, she'd quite liked Loki in the movies. Maybe it'd partly been Tom Hiddleston and his cheeky smile, but she'd always had a soft spot for a villain on a redemption arc. After all, she was hardly a saint.

SEVEN

Left alone in the longhouse, Loki fumed as he could only imagine the battle between Erik's men and Odin's. He wasn't sure what was worse – being forced to watch his fellow warriors cut down, without being able to lift a hand to help them – or not knowing what was happening until the victors returned.

With the witch's spell still binding him, he could neither leave the longhouse or perform magic, but Loki was not entirely unarmed. He had enough henbane to put a man to sleep, and he had a jug of crushed foxglove – enough to make sure a man never woke up.

But when Erik and his men returned, with no sign of Odin, Thor or any of their men…Loki feared the worst. So much for the witch's assurances that Thor would be spared. If it was any consolation to him, Fenrir did not appear among the warriors, either. So if Thor was dead…at least he'd sent one of Erik's men to his death first.

"Snake man!" Erik bellowed. "Bring me the snake man!"

Hands grabbed Loki and dragged him before the high table, where Erik sat among his men. A whole row of red faces told Loki they'd all taken jusquiasmus before the battle, and even now were still feeling the effects. Either that or they'd drunk too much ale, which didn't seem likely as they didn't slur when they called for drink.

Loki refused to bow to his mother's

murderer. "What do you want?"

"Entertain us, snake man! Your people are defeated, and your future depends on my favour. Entertain us, and I will allow you to join us."

Loki wet his lips. He was no singer, and without his magic, none of his usual tricks would work. Which left him with… "I propose a challenge. I challenge your best man to an eating contest. If they win, I will join you." He'd rather die first, but he didn't say that. "And if I win, then I am free to go." Free to leave the hall, transform into a dragon, and burn them all to ash. The least they deserved for killing everyone he'd ever known or loved.

"Where would you go, snake man? There are none of your people left!" Orm taunted.

Let Orm take up the challenge, Loki prayed. If Orm had commanded the attack that killed his mother, then he deserved to die as much as Erik did.

Loki grinned. "What do you care? As long as I no longer have to look at your ugly face, anywhere is better than here."

Laughter roared across the hall. Orm the traitor was not well-liked. The gods help Astrid if Erik did tried to marry her to the man. Perhaps that's why Fenrir wasn't here – he'd spirited her away during the battle. Good luck to them both. As long as she was lost to Erik, Loki's honour was satisfied.

"Are none of you brave enough to challenge a snake to an eating contest?" Loki said.

The older of Erik's two sons stood. "I, Baldur, will accept your challenge, snake man."

Space was made at the table for Loki, and he barely managed to set his foxglove filled cup down before a trencher landed in front of him, topped with pork.

Someone filled his cup with mulled mead before he could stop them, but Loki knew better than to touch the cup, even if it hadn't been poisoned, for to fill his belly with liquid was to lose, he'd learned long ago in contests against Thor.

Baldur had no such qualms. He quaffed his

own cup, then reached for Loki's and downed that, too, his eyes challenging Loki over the brim.

Loki kept his head down and concentrated on the food, hardly daring to look at the man beside him as he called for more mulled mead, draining Loki's refilled cup more times than he could count.

It was the mead that won the contest for him in the end – the crushed foxgloves stewing in the bottom of the cup would not kill Baldur for another day or two yet, as the deadly poison wove its spell through his blood and around his heart. By the time Baldur breathed his last, Loki would be far away from here.

"The snake man is the winner!" the witch cried, as it took two men to carry the unconscious Baldur away from the table.

Erik's other son pounded on the table, his face the reddest of the lot. "Nay, nay! Baldur is not Father's best man, for he drinks too much. I am Father's best man. Name me so, Father, and I shall take up the snake man's challenge.

He has not won until he defeats me!"

The witch frowned, opening her mouth to protest.

Loki jumped up. "I accept the challenge! I ask only for a cup of jusquiasmus to ease my belly before we start!"

"As do I!" the son shouted.

Erik nodded. "Very well, Logi, you shall be my champion against the snake man. Avenge your brother's loss!"

Oh, if only Erik knew. Loki ducked his head to hide his grin.

The witch brought two fresh cups of mead, sprinkling them liberally with jusquiasmus seeds before setting them both on the table before Logi and Loki. "Drink, and then the contest shall start," she said.

Logi grinned and seized both cups, drinking them both down before Loki could react. The fool had already doomed himself, without taking a single bite. Who was Loki to protest his fate?

Two more trenchers, loaded with meat and

vegetables, and they began. Loki was glad he hadn't eaten since the previous day, or he would never have kept up with Erik's son.

Amid the cheers and laughter as Erik's men urged Logi on and taunted Loki, Loki felt eyes on him. Not daring to be too obvious, he allowed himself a quick glance around the hall. In the shadows, by the wall…he could scarcely believe it…Odin sat, with a leather patch over one eye.

Odin lived!

Loki forced himself to take another big bite of food, trencher and all, as he tried to think. He could not burn the hall with everyone inside if Odin was here. He needed to find a way to speak to Odin, to find out how he was here, and whether anyone else had survived. Odin would know what he should do.

But Logi was flagging, the jusquiasmus starting to take effect, on top of all he'd drunk before the battle. If Loki won, Erik would toss him out of the hall, just like he'd asked for, and he wouldn't be able to talk to Odin.

Horror overcame Loki. In order to speak to Odin, he'd have to lose.

Loki reached for his empty cup, and pretended to drink from it, before letting it fall from his fingers as he fell forward onto the table, feigning sleep.

Men shook him as they proclaimed Logi the winner, but Loki just stayed put, keeping his breathing even, until true sleep overcame him.

EIGHT

"What's that supposed to be? It looks like a toddler wrote it! Give that to me!"

Jorunn was only too happy to hand the artefact labels to Nik, who was even less of a saint than she was. Then again, anyone who worked this closely with Nik without strangling him had to be at least halfway to sainthood. She didn't know how Sibyl did it.

She was sorely tempted to ask Sibyl to take

over from her, but she knew she couldn't. This was about watching Nik, seeing if she could find any evidence that he was stealing artefacts.

"I'll take that!" Nik snatched the camera out of Jorunn's hands, as if he didn't trust her with it. Never mind that it was technically her camera, purchased with Harald Medal funds for her research.

"Fine," Jorunn sighed, whipping out her phone to use that instead. It would go faster if they both took pictures, instead of her taking them twice. She paused to make a note in her dictation app, dropping the text into the caption.

Nik had already moved onto the next marker, ripping it out of the rocks that held it. "Nothing here, move onto the next one."

Jorunn stared at the ground. "But there was a marker. There must be something." She dropped into a crouch, carefully brushing away the rocks with her hands. She didn't want to admit it, but Nik had been right. There was nothing here.

"I told you there was nothing. Why will you silly girls not listen?" Nik grumbled as he marched off to the next marker.

Jorunn blew out a frustrated breath. If this had been one of her transects, she'd be able to go through her phone photos and check, but someone else had marked this find. Or whatever they thought they'd seen anyway. Unless someone had just dropped a marker by accident or as a prank…

No, she decided. Everyone here knew better than to waste time like that. They didn't play pranks.

Unless there really was a poltergeist…

She snorted. No, there were no such things as ghosts or Norse gods or anything supernatural. Well, unless you counted the sheer perfection that was Jensen Ackles' arse…

Nik pulled up three more markers, muttering about foolish PhD students and false alarms. "You girls should be sent back to the university, instead of being out in the field with experts who know what they are looking for. These markers have nothing but rocks!"

But this still wasn't her transect, or Sibyl's. She counted the transect paths, trying to remember who'd been in this row. Karl and Lara had taken the outside ones, Lars and Andreas had been between her and Sibyl, Fredrik had walked beside Karl, which left…

"This was your transect. If anyone's planting false markers, it's you, Nik. So shove your complaints up your arse or I'll tell Karl how incompetent you've been today. Got it?" Jorunn growled. She was so sick of his bullshit.

"It will be my word against yours, and who would believe you?" Nik sneered.

Anyone with half a brain who'd been paying attention today, Jorunn wanted to say, but just as she opened her mouth, Karl called for a break.

Jorunn strode away from Nik as fast as she dared over the scree slope, making a beeline for Sibyl, who gave her a sympathetic smile. Jorunn couldn't help but return it.

"If you don't push him off a glacier before

this season ends, I swear I will," Jorunn said.

"Maybe he's right, and I don't belong here. It's not like we've found anything even remotely connected to Utgard. Whereas you've found two hunting arrows already…" Sibyl sighed.

"Three. Found a third one this morning. Three arrows in two weeks is a new record, Karl said." The words were out of her mouth before Jorunn could stop them. Shit.

Another sigh. "If the borders weren't closed, I'd give up and go home to Australia. I'm not cut out for this."

Time to make amends. "Don't talk like that." Jorunn slung an arm around Sibyl's shoulder and gave her a supporting squeeze. "We're the first ever dual Harald Medal winners. The only two in a decade. Hundreds of candidates entered, and they picked us. We're the best there is. Saint Nik never won a medal. He's just jealous, not to mention bitter that it's our prize money that's funding this entire expedition. He wouldn't even be here if it weren't for us. We've only been out here two weeks. I bet your Buggerup dig didn't find anything in the first two weeks, either. We've got three arrows, and a bunch of other stuff."

Sibyl managed a watery smile. "Burrup, not Buggerup. And yeah, it took them three years of underwater survey work to find a site as rich as the one they finally did locate."

"Maybe we should push Saint Nik in the lake, and see if he finds anything interesting there." Even better, hold him under for a while and hope he drank some prehistoric bug in the lake water that gave him some agonising illness.

"He'd probably make us do his laundry while he sulks in his tent until his gear is dry. Or insist on borrowing our gear instead," Sibyl said.

Ugh, doing Nik's laundry while he had some ghastly gastro bug? Jorunn wanted to gag. "And he wouldn't wash it before he gave it back, either. Imagine having to wear your gear after he'd sweated in it for days, unwashed.

Just kill me now."

"Only if you'd do the same for me," Sibyl said.

Things had gotten really bad if they were making death pacts. Jorunn would have to try harder to cheer up her roommate.

"Or…I could help you wish the dishes tonight, after dinner, and when everyone's gone to bed, you could help me liberate a bottle of Lara's aquavit and we could share it in the tent later. What do you say?" Jorunn asked. She'd forgotten to grab the bottle yesterday, or they'd be able to head straight to the tent.

Sibyl bit her lip. "You found an arrow today. That means you've won a night off doing the dishes. Plus…aren't those bottles all we have for the whole trip? What if Lara notices one missing?"

Jorunn opened her mouth to tell Sibyl she already had Lara's permission, but Andreas walked past, and she didn't want anyone else thinking they could just help themselves to the alcohol stash. They'd be out in three days — she'd seen how much those guys could drink. "They're for medicinal purposes. If she asks, I'll tell her Saint Nik was sapping our will to live, and nothing would restore it except some water of life. She'll understand. Besides, with the expedition budget higher than usual, we have a regular supply run. Jakop and his horses will be back in no time, and she can always order more for the next trip."

"All right, then," Sibyl said, like she was still agreeing to a death pact.

Jorunn tried harder. "Ah, the day's not even half over. Who knows? This afternoon, we might find one of Hemsworth's ancestors, complete with a hammer as big as he is, and he'll take one look at Saint Nik and pound him so deep into a glacier, no one will find him for a hundred years." Or Loki could turn up and turn him into…a lemming or something. She could probably handle Nik as a lemming. Especially if a bird swooped out of nowhere and tried to eat him…

"I think you're thinking of Captain America. He's the one who vanished beneath the Arctic ice and woke up much later."

Wait, what? It took Jorunn a moment to remember what they'd been talking about. Oh yeah, superheroes. Definitely not hot villains. "But he was a hot blonde dude, right?"

Sibyl laughed. "Yeah, he was that, too."

Maybe Sibyl hadn't noticed her daydreaming and getting all distracted. This was about cheering Sibyl up, and maybe herself as well. "Well, that's what they do with superhero movies, isn't it? They mash up all the stories into one movie-length one? So who says we won't find Thor holding his hammer, ready to jump to defend your reputation as an archaeologist? Maybe if we drink enough aquavit, he will!"

Sibyl sighed. "All right, all right. Dishes and drinks tonight, whether we find something amazing or nothing at all. Deal?"

"Only if you promise not to talk about leaving again. You're the only one keeping me sane out here," Jorunn said. Or from killing Nik. Maybe she should tell Sibyl about her suspicions. Just in case…

"It's a deal," Sibyl said.

"Right." Jorunn looked around, realising the others were lining up for transects again. She should probably join then, instead of working with Nik. Even after a whole morning of watching him like one of the eagles that occasionally flew overhead, she still had no evidence he'd been stealing stuff. Maybe the arsehole was actually innocent. "Back to work."

NINE

Green and purple streaked the sky, just like arctic foxes running through snow. That's what Thor's mother, Jord, had said those lights were, while his father, Hymir, had feared them. Loki's own mother had told him they were no more dangerous than the moon and stars in the sky, and that no one had ever been harmed by them.

Yet Loki could hear a man screaming…

Thor, his befuddled mind told him. The last time he'd heard Thor scream like that was when he'd turned Thor's belt into a sea serpent, the one thing the warrior feared.

Loki sat up, desperate to see if it was true, whether Thor still lived.

Just in time to see Astrid lift Thor's dripping heart from his chest, as his screams vanished into silence.

Loki could not believe he'd been so blind. He'd poisoned Erik's sons, but in allowing this girl to live, presumably carried off by Fenrir, he'd made a grave error. He should have bitten her when she'd first seized him in the longhouse. Then Thor might still be alive…

"The sacrifice is now complete. He is now a protector who awaits my call," the girl said. "Protector Thor, what will you do when you hear my call?"

He's dead, you crazy bitch. He can't answer your stupid call, Loki wanted to scream, but Kun's spell still lingered, not letting him make a sound.

Thor's eyes flew open. "I will answer your call, and fight at your command, mistress."

Thor, turning traitor? Loki would not believe it. Could not believe it. Yet Thor needed no spell on him to make sure every word he uttered was the truth. Then why…how…?

"Will you protect me?" the girl continued.

"I am yours to command, mistress," Thor said.

It had to be a spell of some sort.

He watched, helpless, as Erik's men lifted Thor and lowered him into a grave. Loki glimpsed runes daubed across Thor's chest before he disappeared from sight.

He glanced down. He, too, had the same runes daubed across his chest in sticky, red ink that he knew had to be blood. He turned his head, trying to read them.

Oh, gods, that one said obey, didn't it? And serve… That's what had turned Thor into a thrall. Loki scrubbed desperately at the runes, trying to smear them before the girl could finish the spell. Was this what Kun had talked about — turning Odin's men into ensorcelled stone protectors, like the ones who'd destroyed his village?

Loki would rather die than kill at Erik's command…or the command of this slip of a girl he should have killed the moment he met her…

"That one next." When the girl pointed at him, Loki quickly lay back down and closed his eyes, trying to cover the smudged runes with his arm so she didn't notice.

Hands held him down, pressing him against the icy ground.

"That's up to Odin, daughter. What do you say, Odin? The other one is a strong warrior, obedient and willing to serve. But this one…he's a traitor. He betrayed you, telling my men everything when they caught him, to preserve his own miserable life, for little more than a bag of gold and jewels." A clinking bag landed on Loki's belly, and it took all Loki's determination not to grab it and smash Erik's face with it. "He's the reason we were waiting when you emerged from the pass. He's my man, not yours. Would you trust him enough to command him in battle, or shall I just cut out his heart and leave it for the wolves?"

Loki opened his eyes, to meet Erik's. He could see the knife out of the corner of his eye, poised to stab into his runed chest, but Loki had the courage of Thor and the conviction of Odin in that moment. "Do it," he hissed. "I'm no traitor. I'd rather die than serve you."

The blade pierced Loki's chest, the pain so intense for a moment before everything went black.

TEN

Okay, maybe Jorunn shouldn't have drunk so much last night. She'd rarely had any alcohol in Australia – seeing as if she brought any home, her mother was sure to drink it before Jorunn could – but she'd probably had more to drink here in Norway than she had for the entirety of last year at home. Some pain pills went a long way to sorting her headache, though, and it wasn't like she'd drunk herself unconscious, like Mum. Even Sibyl, who looked seriously hungover this morning, hadn't had that much aquavit.

Maybe they should go easy on the stuff tonight, or avoid it altogether.

One thing Jorunn did know for certain: she had no patience for Nik, or his insults today, so she stuck to transects.

Until a gleam between the rocks caught her eye, and she knelt down for a closer look. Her breath caught in her throat.

This was no corroded coin – it was gold, as bright and new as the day it was first minted. Automatically, Jorunn pulled out her phone and GPS to document the find before picking it up and snapping a few more pictures from different angles as she examined it.

It was a brooch as big as her palm, made of golden amber set in heavy gold. The soft metal still showed signs of runes or some sort of design carved into it, almost polished smooth by the ice. Whoever had owned this had been someone important, for certain. Even now, it would be worth a fortune.

And if someone — mostly likely Nik — was stealing artefacts, they'd definitely drool over this one. It'd be gone before Jorunn could blink.

So she couldn't put it back on the ground, beside a marker. She'd have to sneak it into the artefact boxes in the mess tent, somehow, hidden under something else, so Nik or whoever the thief was didn't find it.

Jorunn rose to her feet, glancing around to make sure no one was watching, then set off along her transect path again, as though she'd found nothing of interest. After a moment, she slipped the brooch into her pocket.

She forgot about it until lunch, when she sat down on a rock and heard a clink as it slipped out of her pocket onto the ground.

"Shit." She scooped it up and tried to put it away again.

"I knew it was a mistake to let an Aussie girl like you come on such an important expedition," Nik hissed, appearing out of nowhere.

If the Norse gods, or any deity was listening, she needed their help now. If Nik noticed the brooch…

"I'll tell you what. You give that to me right now, and I won't tell Karl I saw you stealing it."

That was rich, coming from him. "I wasn't…" she exploded.

"I saw you put it in your pocket. But I might forget about that if you do something for me. How about it?" He gave her what he probably thought was a charming smile. It just made her feel ill.

Now she could barely keep her lunch down. "But I didn't…" she began, then had to close her mouth before her lunch made a second appearance. She didn't like salmon usually, and choking it down the first time had been hard enough. Bringing it back up again…

"Look, girl, either I tell Karl I saw you stealing artefacts from the dig, or you come and share my tent tonight. Deal?"

Sleep with Nik?

Jorunn lost the battle with the salmon, and threw up on Nik's boots.

ELEVEN

Waves bashed the headland, but in the lee of it, fish clustered. That's where Loki dropped his hook, because he knew he'd catch plenty. Enough for the whole week, if he was lucky. Mother would be pleased with him then, and maybe Father would let him come out on the fishing boat with him, instead of leaving him ashore with the women and children. He was more than capable of shouldering a man's load. He knew it, but his father kept putting him off. Next week and next month and next year…as though he did not want his son to be aboard the ship with him. As though Loki wasn't every bit as good a fisherman as his father, if not better.

Something took the bait and suddenly Loki had to hold fast to his line, lest he lose it, fish and all. But he held on, and kept pulling, until his catch breached the surface.

Only to find it was his father's head…

Loki woke with a start. A dream – it had to be a dream. He hadn't been fishing once since the day he'd lost his family, and he had no intention of fishing ever again.

Help.

The whispered word sent a surge of blood rushing through him, the need to rise, to protect…

Ridiculous decisions, if he chose to make them. He was not Erik's slave, ensorcelled by his witches. He was a shapeshifter, and he answered the call of the wild, not some woman. He could be anything he wanted, do anything he wanted.

And right now, he wanted to go back to sleep.

And yet…he couldn't. For the woman was still there, and she was not alone.

"I'll tell you what. You give that to me right now, and I won't tell Karl I saw you stealing it."

"I wasn't…"

"I saw you put it in your pocket. But I might forget about that if you do something for me. How about it?"

Loki didn't like this man. Too slimy by half.

"But I didn't…"

"Look, girl, either I tell Karl I saw you stealing artefacts from the dig, or you come and share my tent tonight. Deal?"

Help. The word came from her, even stronger, even though she didn't say a word.

And the man, whose whiny voice reminded Loki of a mosquito…

He shot through the stone, searching. Ah,

there they were — swarms and swarms of them, just waiting to be unleashed. And he did, sending them toward the slimy man.

Who moved off, leaving Loki and the unnamed woman in peace.

Thank you. Her words echoed in his head, unsaid and yet definitely said, as she briefly sported an embarrassed smile just for him, before turning back to her task — looking for treasures in the rocks, like the one she'd found that the slimy man wanted, whatever it was.

Loki glimpsed it for only a moment, but it was enough to freeze his heart in his chest.

That was Odin's cloak pin. The one that had belonged to his wife, which he hadn't taken off since the day she died, and he'd laid a bunch of wilted roses on her pyre before it all burned. If his cloak pin was here, then he was here. Somewhere.

Alive, just as Loki himself was.

Did he still think Loki was a traitor, after hearing Erik's lies? Or would he listen to Loki's own explanation for what had happened?

Loki had to find him, and tell him, and hope…

Yes. He had his own honour to save.

He'd get the pin back from the thief, and bring it to Odin as a gift. A peace offering.

Hearing her voice in his head must be part of the spell he hadn't managed to entirely shake off. But he could resist it. He didn't need to obey Erik, or Erik's thief. He could steal the brooch back from her, with no qualms whatsoever.

Because to do Erik's bidding was to truly be a traitor, and he had to prove to Odin he was as loyal now as he was the day Odin had put his spear into his hand. As loyal as he'd always been, no matter what Erik said.

TWELVE

Sibyl looked as green as Jorunn felt, but she stood up, ready to continue the survey when Karl called, so Jorunn had no excuse but to go back to work, too.

Until Sibyl said, "Guys, I think I found something." That catch in her voice grabbed everyone's attention, even before they saw the hammer.

The rest of the day was a blur, as they gave

up the survey to pry the hammer from the ice. The energy in the air, the eagerness to be part of such a discovery…Jorunn could almost taste it. And when they carried the hammer back to the mess tent…everyone wanted to hold the tub.

She and Sibyl trailed after the procession, more stunned than hungover at this point.

Dinner was a distracted affair, with everyone shooting glances at the ice block that gave them tantalising glimpses of the hammer as it melted.

Until Jorunn realised she still had that bloody brooch in her pocket. Well, the mess tent was the place to hide it, with all the other artefacts. She edged toward the boxes in the corner, and slipped the brooch under the lid of the topmost one while no one was watching.

Then a chunk of ice calved off the hammer, landing with a mighty splash in the tub below.

"Oh my god, you really found Thor's hammer!" Jorunn cried, hugging Sibyl. It wasn't Utgard, but it was still an amazing find.

She had to stay now.

Karl sent everyone off with orders to have an early night, as they had a lot of documentation work to do tomorrow before the packhorses arrived to take the first load of artefacts back to the university for safekeeping.

Which meant she needed to label the brooch now, before someone discovered it and started asking questions. Jorunn dug out one of the documentation cards, and pulled out her phone. As long as she got the GPS location right, no one would mind if the rest of the card wasn't filled out.

Then she opened the artefact box where she'd stashed the brooch…and it wasn't there.

"What are you doing?"

Jorunn nearly dropped the box in shock at Karl's demand.

"I was trying to put the documentation with one of today's finds, only it's not here," she said. She held out the card, then pulled out her phone to show him the picture of the brooch. "See? I know I put it in here, but I found the card, and realised I hadn't attached it, so I came back to fix things."

"Came back to steal it, I bet," Nik snarled.

She hadn't even seen him enter the mess tent.

"No, I didn't. It was here," she protested.

"Turn out your pockets!" Nik demanded.

Fuck. It was like she was six years old again, being shouted at for doing what Mum said. Only this time, she knew she was innocent.

Slowly, Jorunn pulled things out of her coat pockets. A lip balm. Her head torch. Two spare hair ties. A silicon sachet that must have still been in there since she bought the coat. A spare power pack to charge her phone out in the field that she hadn't had to use today, what with all the excitement over the hammer. Nothing that shouldn't be there, and definitely not the brooch that had been there for half the day.

"Your pants pockets, too!" Nik barked.

Jorunn set her hands on her hips. "They're women's pants, dickhead. They're not made to stuff a couple of pairs of socks down the front to make yourself look impressive. Women's pants don't have pockets big enough for anything bigger than a lip balm, and even if I did have one in there, which I don't, you'd see it. See?" She grabbed the one on the table and shoved it in her pocket, where it stuck out, pressed against her hip bone.

Karl held up a hand. "Enough. Put your things away, Jorunn, and then would you step outside with me for a minute? Nikolai, you stay here."

"You bet I will. I must make sure she does not steal anything else," Nik muttered, grabbing a chair and setting it beside the stacked artefact boxes, before he seated himself, folding his arms like he was some sort of bouncer or guard. Poser.

Jorunn shoved her stuff back in her coat pocket, and followed Karl out into the night air. Was it just her, or had the temperature dropped ten degrees?

Karl sighed. "Look, Jorunn, I know this is

very new to you, but remote archaeology like this is very much a matter of teamwork. We work hard together to uncover history that's been hidden for hundreds or even thousands of years, fighting weather and climate change and whatever else Mother Nature throws at us to make it even harder. It's important that we all get along, and we do not disrespect each other."

"He was being a dickhead! He called me a thief!" Jorunn protested. God, she sounded like a whiny six-year-old. She wasn't Jojo any more. She wasn't.

"Things have been going missing from the site. While it's possible they've just been mislaid, it's increasingly likely that there is a thief on this expedition. And after I saw you smuggle a bottle of aquavit out under your jacket last night…"

"Lara said I could take it. I just didn't want anyone else to see it," she began. "Honestly, if you're pointing fingers at anyone, it's Saint Nik you should be suspicious of. I've found coins almost every day we've been out, and yet there isn't a single one in the artefact boxes. The only person documenting our finds on every single one of those days is Nik."

Karl didn't believe her. Even though it was the truth. God, if she had half the wheedling persuasiveness of her mother, he'd be lapping up every word and arresting Nik on the spot.

Karl sighed. "Like I said, this expedition is about all of us working together to discover the secrets of the past. Not hiding them or disagreeing with each other. Once the expedition is over, you can both write papers to every peer reviewed journal out there, disputing the findings and conclusions of what we find for the rest of your professional lives. But now, we work together. Nikolai is your colleague. Those artefacts are priceless national treasures that belong to the world, and the museum is waiting for them. Will you help me in ensuring no more of them go missing?"

In other words, would she please stop stealing them, Jorunn thought but didn't say.

Damn it. Karl was actually a nice guy. One her mother would rob blind, given half a chance, and one who was being robbed blind by someone else – most likely Nik, if she could only find the proof.

Which gave her the answer Karl wanted. "Absolutely. I'll do everything I can to make sure everything we find here makes it safely to the lab, and then on to the museum," she said. Even if she had to hold Nik upside down and shake him to empty his pockets.

Karl gave her a tired smile. "I'm delighted to hear it. Now, bed. For you and for me." He trudged off toward his tent.

THIRTEEN

Despite the direct order from the leader of this little encampment, the thief headed for the tent they were using as a yard house. Loki debated whether to confront her inside the close confines, or wait until she emerged. While the first would be funnier, he decided the second would be more practical. He didn't want to risk her dropping the brooch into the cesspit if he startled her, which he certainly would if he burst in on her doing her ablutions.

Perhaps he should do more to set her at her ease, so she'd hand the brooch over without trouble. He'd watched the encampment for long enough to know the men wore different garb to his own. If he looked like one of them, she was more likely to trust him. He could steal clothing from one of the men, but they were all in their tents, so that might prove difficult. Easier to create the illusion of such clothing instead.

"Who the fuck are you?"

While he'd been distracted, trying to perfect the illusion, she'd emerged.

Loki straightened. This would have to do. "I am a traveller, recently arrived across the pass, and I wish to share your fire for the night."

She raised her eyebrows. "That's a line I haven't heard before. Don't you know this is a national park, where fires aren't allowed?"

That…was not possible. "How did you and your people cook your food, then?" he demanded. He'd smelled the hot meal, and while he'd heard of people to the north, whose mountains spat fire and smoke, cooking their food in hot springs that steamed like cauldrons, he saw no signs of such things here.

She looked uncomfortable. "We have permission to use a couple of gas cookers, but we only have a limited amount of gas, and if we run out, it's trail mix and tinned sardines until the next supply run, or at least that's what Lara threatened us with when one of the guys left the stove on."

Loki barely understood a word of this. "But I am a traveller. Is it not customary to offer me hospitality?"

She laughed. "First you want to use our stove, and now you're asking for space in my tent? Dude, even Saint Nik's offer was better than that, and he still got a "fuck no" response. What the hell are you doing up here in the mountains without proper gear?"

This was not going as well as he had hoped. "I am a simple traveller…"

"Yeah, you said that, and it still makes no sense. No one comes up here except the archaeology teams, because this is a protected site. And as you're not one of us…you're not here for anything good. Which makes me wonder…are you the thief who's been stealing our stuff?"

After Erik had called him a traitor, now his drudge called him a thief? Loki had never been so insulted in his life. He drew himself up to his full height. "I, Loki Laufeyjarson, am many things, but I am not and have never been a thief."

If anything, this only seemed to make her even more suspicious. "You say your name is Loki? Really Loki?"

A rustling sound, before a man emerged from a nearby tent. "Hey, Jorunn. You going to use the WC, or is it free?"

The thief – the real thief – turned away. "Oh, hey, Fredrik. No, I'm done. It's all yours."

She turned back to Loki…or where Loki

had been standing, before he'd slipped beneath the stones at her feet. Not a moment too soon, or this Fredrik would have seen him.

The thief hurried back to her tent before Loki could follow.

Loki cursed foolish Fredrik and his weak bladder for interrupting him. He'd been this close to demanding the brooch from her. Another moment and it might already be in his hands…

Next time, he would succeed, Loki promised himself. The thief could not be allowed to keep Odin's brooch.

FOURTEEN

Now that was seriously weird. Last night, after sharing half a bottle of aquavit with Sibyl, she might possibly have hallucinated Loki while stumbling to or from the loo in the middle of the night. But tonight, she'd been so stinking sober, she wished she'd been hallucinating all of it. The brooch disappearing, then the accusations from Karl and Nik, and as for…seriously, Loki?

Perhaps her tired brain had accidentally hit on the truth in there somewhere.

Maybe, just maybe, the Norse gods did actually exist, and were still listening in places like this, where their worshippers had lived for so long. And maybe the trickster among them had decided to come and create a little chaos among the archaeologists. Throw around a few coins, a bunch of arrows, and a beautiful brooch that definitely didn't belong in a remote mountain pass.

Before asking her for dinner and sex. Well, maybe not sex…he might have been literal, in asking for a bed for the night. Vikings all slept together in longhouses, after all, so maybe that sort of thing hadn't come across as quite as dickish back then as it did now.

But the way he'd grinned and the heat in his eyes as he'd asked for a hospitality…even if he hadn't been asking for sex, he'd definitely been thinking about it.

Luckily, the sensible part of her brain had managed to articulate a firm FUCK NO, but now she had time to consider it…

Well, of course she wasn't going to sleep with a guy she'd just met, who'd wandered into the camp out of nowhere, before vanishing into nothing. Even if he was Loki, the god of…what was he the god of, anyway? Wasn't it mischief or something?

She wouldn't mind getting up to mischief with him…

Okay, she'd always had a soft spot for the Marvel character, or maybe it was just Tom Hiddleston, who looked nothing like the guy she'd just met outside the freaking toilet, of all places, but he had said he was Loki Laufeyjarson, and wasn't that what the dude from the movies had been called? Laufey something, anyway. It wasn't like Loki was a common name here in Norway, unlike Thor or Jan.

It was a damn good thing she had Sibyl for a roommate. Even if she was tempted to bring some guy back to their tent (who might or might not be an actual god), no way was she getting up to any kind of mischief with Sibyl right there next to her.

Sibyl, who was too nice and sweet to have a one night stand in her life. Living with a family she loved and sometimes got homesick for, she'd have taken one look at Loki and run away screaming.

Whereas Jorunn fantasised about running away with him…

Inside the tent, Sibyl was fast asleep. Probably dreaming about marrying Thor, after finding his hammer under the ice today. Because Sibyl was definitely the marrying kind.

Only…what on earth was that draped over her sleeping bag? It looked a bit like that tunic Saint Nik kept banging on about, the one he'd found here on a previous expedition. Only a whole lot bigger…

"Sibyl! Sibyl!"

Sibyl clenched her eyes shut even tighter. "Unless your name is Thor and you have more muscles than a Hemsworth, all the better to carry me away to your castle in the sky, go away."

Ha! So she had been dreaming of Thor! "You can go back to dreaming about hot Vikings as soon as you tell me where and how you got that."

"Got what?" Sibyl grumbled, sitting up.

Jorunn's jaw dropped. Sibyl hadn't been injured earlier, but now she looked like she'd been in the wars.

"And that!"

"Jorunn…" Sibyl began, sounding almost annoyed. "I have no idea what you're talking about."

A blow to the head could cause some memory loss. Even Jorunn knew that. Jorunn took a deep breath. "Well, first, that epic wool blanket that I've never seen before, which you couldn't possibly have carried in your backpack here. And then there's the bloodstained bandage wrapped around your head. Even if you have been fighting Vikings in your dreams, it still doesn't explain that."

One hand went to her head, while the other

stretched out to stroke the blanket. Sibyl looked like she might remember something, and it was definitely the stuff of dreams, not nightmares.

Jorunn pulled off the bandage and dropped it in Sibyl's lap. "I suppose you're going to tell me that's not your blood, but someone else's."

Sibyl lifted a tentative hand to her head and winced at the blood that now coated her fingers. "No, I think it's mine. I slipped and hit my head earlier when I…when I went to the bathroom," she said.

If Loki had attacked her roommate, Jorunn was going to tear him a new one. God or not, no one messed with her friends.

But that didn't explain the cloak on Sibyl's bed. Or the bandage.

Besides, Sibyl hadn't mentioned Loki. She'd been dreaming about Thor.

"I suppose Thor himself materialised, carried you back here, and gave you his cloak as a souvenir so you'd know he was real?" Jorunn said, not sure whether to laugh, or begin to believe it. After all, if she'd really met Loki…was it such a stretch for Sibyl to encounter Thor?

"I don't remember," Sibyl said, looking bewildered. She climbed out of bed and looked down at her slippers, which she was still wearing under her coat. Sibyl never wore those to bed – even in subzero temperatures, she changed into a pair of pyjamas and bedsocks every night.

Sibyl pressed her lips together tightly, as if trying to stop them from trembling, and grabbed the cloak. "I'm going to the bathroom," she said.

What was she going to do with the cloak? Use it for toilet paper? Jorunn was afraid to ask, so instead, she said, "Don't hit your head again, then. Or I'll have to get Nik to help me carry you back here. I definitely couldn't do it myself."

Sibyl just nodded vaguely and stepped outside.

"Whoever owns this cloak, show yourself

right now, or I'll burn it to ash," she said softly, as if she was afraid of who might respond.

Jorunn crept to the door of their tent, ready to jump to Sibyl's aid if Loki returned. After a moment's thought, she picked up the half empty aquavit bottle from last night. She'd smash it over Loki's head if she had to. Fair punishment for hurting Sibyl's head.

Footsteps crunched on the rocks outside. Sibyl's…or someone else's?

Then a man's deep voice said, "You appeared cold, mistress, and you had no cloak of your own, so I covered you with mine. I realise it is not fine enough for a lady like yourself, but it was all I had, and I am sworn to protect you in all things, even from something as mundane as the cold air."

Was this man for real? If he was, Sibyl would definitely be swooning about now. Even Jorunn was feeling a little misty.

"You can't be real. You can't be," Sibyl said.

The deep, sexy voice spoke again: "I assure

you, mistress, I am Thor, your sworn protector, and both I and all I possess are at your service. Please, wear my cloak to keep you warm, until I can provide you with one that is far finer and more fitting for your station."

Yes. YES! Jorunn fist-pumped in triumph. If Thor was real, then so was Loki, and if she saw him again, she was definitely going to reconsider that hospitality thing. Hadn't Sibyl said something about a castle in the sky? She didn't need a whole castle, just a room with a big bed…

"You can't be Thor. You don't have a hammer," Sibyl said matter-of-factly, smashing Jorunn's fantasy into pieces.

A long pause. Then, "I seem to have mislaid it," he said. "I will find a suitable weapon before sunset on the morrow, so that I might better protect you" Another pause. "I will protect you, mistress. I swear it, from now until my last breath. If you could persuade the other witch to return my hammer, I would use it solely in your service."

Wait – there was a witch here, too? First Loki, now Thor…was the entire Norse pantheon here?

Shit. Jorunn sat down heavily on her bed, then had to lie down. This was definitely more than she'd signed up for.

FIFTEEN

Loki paced along the lakeshore, needing the space and the movement to think, but his mind was awhirl with so many thoughts, he wasn't sure what to think.

The thief was the servant of one of Erik's witches — a slip of a girl he'd never seen before, but Loki knew better than to measure magical power by size. Erik's Eastern witch Kun had been small, but he'd never known a witch that powerful.

Worse, this new witch had awakened Thor…and now the fool thought he was her protector. Which meant if Loki wanted to get to the thief, he had to get through Thor and a witch. Wonderful.

Loki should have been paying more attention to his surroundings, or he'd have noticed the juggernaut bearing down on him before it bowled him over, pinning him to the rocky ground.

"You stole my hammer! I know it was you! Return it at once!"

Ensorcelled Thor was one thing, but a second accusation of theft in one night? Loki had had enough. "I haven't touched your hammer," Loki snapped. "That thing's too big to be of use to anyone. Why you don't use an axe like a normal warrior…"

Of course, Thor would not ignore an insult to his weapon. "That was my father's weapon, made from a dying star. I've killed more men with it in a day than you have in your entire life. Just because you are too weak to lift it…"

Loki waited for Thor to finish the litany he'd heard a hundred times before. Thor might be enslaved by Erik and his witches, but he never forgot his weapon's history.

Finally, Thor finished with, "Tell me where you have hidden it, so we can both protect our new mistress together, as brothers in arms once more."

Gods. The spell had rotted Thor's brain. "I would rather die than serve that witch. I'm no traitor. I only wish I had taken your hammer, so that I might use it to knock some sense into you. We are Odin's men, not Erik's, no matter what spell that witch cast. You shouldn't be protecting her, you should be killing her, along with Erik and all his men."

Thor's eyes widened in horror. "No. Our mistress is not Erik's daughter, but a different witch. One far more powerful. She had a crown with a living star that glows. We must protect her," he said.

Not for the first time, Loki wished he had

magic like his mother, or one of Erik's witches. Aside from a few minor spells, all he could really do was shapeshift and cast illusions. Useful in their own way, but also utterly useless in the face of this curse that afflicted Thor.

"You sound like a fool. You do mean the girl who slipped on the ice, without the wit to wear proper boots or even a cloak against the cold? Whatever she's done to make you think she has power, you're wrong. It's a trick, I tell you, and the sooner you see through it, the sooner you will be free of her influence, as I am. You don't see me carrying her about the place, or standing outside in the cold outside her tent!"

Thor's grip on Loki's throat tightened. "If you seek to harm her, I will not allow it. Though you are my brother in arms, and the closest thing I have to a blood brother, I will cut you down where you stand before you can lay a hand on her," Thor growled.

The only magic Loki had left was the power

of persuasion, which had never had much effect on Thor, for he was far too stubborn once he'd made his mind up. "Fine. You are under the witch's spell. You'll feel like even more of a fool when I find out how to break it. You always did have a soft spot for pretty women. Teaching your sister to fight was the most foolish thing you ever did, until today." He meant to remind Thor that Erik and his witches were responsible for Sif's death, but Thor's clenched fist cut off his air so he could no longer speak.

"Sif is now feasting in Valhalla, the best any warrior could hope for. Say one more word about Sif and it will be the last thing you ever say," Thor snarled, before releasing Loki's throat.

Loki rolled his eyes. "So now your sister is a better warrior than both of us put together. Happy now?"

Thor looked torn. Either he could admit a girl was a better warrior than himself, or he'd be the one to insult her. Finally, he said, "You might be right. She would be pleased to hear you say that."

And just like that, the argument was over. Thor might be hot tempered, but he didn't hold a grudge.

Loki clambered to his feet, surprised to find he didn't hurt the way he used to after Thor had gotten the better of him in a fight. He brushed the mud off his clothes. "So what are you going to do now?"

Thor might seem reasonable now, but Loki was under no illusions that he'd broken the spell. He'd need a witch for that.

"You're going to help me search for a suitable weapon that I can use until I find my hammer again. Once I have that, I'm going to go back to watching over the witch, as I swore I would," Thor said, far too smugly for Loki's liking. "Then you may do as you wish."

"I can promise you I won't be serving some strange woman, no matter how pretty she is," Loki said. He thought of the thieving servant girl. The pretty servant girl, he had to admit.

He wouldn't mind taking her for a tumble. If he made sure she enjoyed it, she might even offer the brooch to him in thanks. Of course, he couldn't do it while Thor or his witch were around…but Loki could wait. The gods only knew how long he and Thor had slumbered before they woke. A few more days would do no harm.

SIXTEEN

Jorunn couldn't believe Sibyl was gone. When she'd told Karl about Sibyl's head injury, she'd expected him to order her to rest, get some first aid, and that would be it. Not that he'd send her on a donkey back to civilisation, and not to come back until she had medical clearance to work.

Jorunn's only consolation was that Karl had promised to send the hammer to the lab with her, so even if Sibyl couldn't rejoin the expedition, she could make a start on her PhD research in the meantime.

But that left Jorunn alone in the tent at night, with no one to talk or joke with.

Lara and Karl were lovely, but they were the expedition leaders, her superiors more than her colleagues. Andreas, Fredrik and Lars were all undergraduate students who'd joined the expedition as part of their summer field school requirements, or for extra credit. They were all nice enough guys, if a bit young for her, but that was kind of the point. They made her feel old, when she wasn't, because she was a PhD student and technically their superior, who could ask them to do whatever menial tasks made her research easier. The Harald Medal funding had paid for them, too.

Which left...bloody Saint Nik, who seemed to lurk around her tent more than ever, even though his was at the other end of camp. She didn't trust him, especially without Sibyl here.

Of course, when she'd asked him what he

was doing, he'd airily insisted he was just checking the solar panels, before sauntering off. Slimy bastard.

She'd even gone to the trouble of using a cable tie to lock her tent zipper shut when she went to bed that night. Of course, that meant plenty of swearing in the middle of the night when she wanted to visit the toilet tent, trying to undo the damn thing, but eventually she managed it and stumbled out into the dark, her headtorch slicing a lonely beam of light through the frosty air.

Everything was silent and still as her footsteps crunched across the camp back to her tent, until she turned her head toward the tent itself. A hulking shape stood outside – definitely too big to be Sibyl or Lara, which meant it had to be a man.

If it was Nik, trying to bully her into sleeping with him again so he'd drop his ridiculous accusations…

"Well met, inhospitable maiden," the figure said, turning.

Her hammering heart slowed as she blew out the most relieved breath of her life. "Loki," she said.

"The gods frown upon those who do not offer hospitality to travellers. I'd hoped I might persuade you to reconsider…" he began.

Yes, yes, a thousand times yes. She hadn't believed him the first time they'd met, but now she knew he really was Loki, the god of mischief, no way was she going to miss such an opportunity again.

She threw her arms around his neck and kissed him.

SEVENTEEN

Loki had intended to seduce the girl, but he wasn't going to protest when she threw herself at him, before dragging him inside her tent.

He eyed the empty beds. "Will the witch you serve be returning soon?" If she was, he'd better hurry.

The girl snorted. "Are you talking about my roommate, Sibyl? She's too nice to be a witch. But if you're worried about her coming in and interrupting us, don't. She's headed back to base camp for a medical. She won't be back for weeks."

"And she didn't take her tent or her servant with her? Strange," he said.

She frowned. "Jakop has travelling tents, so she didn't need this one. And the undergrads are research assistants, not servants. Sure, they're the lowest rank on the totem pole here and they kind of do take orders from the rest of us, but they're not...I'm going to go out on a limb here and say you haven't spent much time around people for a while, have you?"

Loki dropped the illusion of clothing like her people wore. Her eyebrows rose a little, but she did not seem as shocked as he thought she might. "I believe I have slept for some time," he admitted.

She looked him up and down, her gaze lingering on his chest and belly.

The blood runes had faded or washed away, but he could still feel them, burning beneath his skin. Perhaps she could see or sense them, too. "Are you the witch's apprentice?" That would explain it.

She sighed. "Sibyl is not a witch, and nor am I. We're both PhD students. Colleagues of equal rank. Scholars who read and write about our research findings. If you're looking for a witch, we don't really have people like that any more."

Loki nodded, absorbing this information, or at least as much of it as he understood. She used many strange words. "I do not wish for a witch. I came here for you."

"And what would Loki, the god of mischief, want with me?"

Loki couldn't help it. He grinned. No one had ever called him the god of anything before, and he rather liked it. "Well, another kiss would be a good start."

"You've been asleep for around a thousand years, and when you woke up, the first thing you thought was, 'Hey, I'd like to fuck Jorunn.'"

Ah, so that was her name. His smile didn't

falter. "Only if you are willing, Jorunn. I promise I will transport you to peaks of pleasure such as you have never known."

A wry smile lifted her lips. "That does sound good. Pity we're here in a freezing cold tent instead of someplace with a big fire and an even bigger bed."

He remembered her saying fires were not allowed in this place, or he'd have lit one for her on the spot. But he did know one charm that was almost as effective…he bit his lip, and willed the tent to become a warm bubble.

She stared at him as she tugged off her coat. "If I could do that, I'd probably walk around with a lot less clothes on, too."

Most women he'd known had been shocked that a man could perform magic, when it was usually only women who were witches. Yet Jorunn did not seem surprised at all. Perhaps she already knew – if she served Erik, he'd likely have told her. Though if she was a scholar and not a witch or a warrior, Erik would have no interest in her…Loki shook his head. What she was and who she served did not matter right now. What mattered was her eager smile and the invitation in her eyes. Erik and all his men be damned. Tonight there was no one else in the world but him and Jorunn.

Loki dragged the beds together, then unfastened his cloak and laid it over the top of them both. "Two of your wishes granted – warmth, and a bigger bed. What else would you ask of me?"

A wistful smile, like she didn't believe she'd receive her desire. "Well, those peaks of pleasure sounded good…"

This time, he took her in his arms and kissed her. Her lips were sweet and soft, yielding far more readily than any woman he'd known before. Her clothes – the unfamiliar fastenings stymied him until she began to help him – soon puddled on the floor, and she reached out to unfasten his trousers.

"Not yet," he said, setting his hands on her bare shoulders. "Sit down on the edge of the bed."

He dropped to his knees before her, gliding one hand up her inner thigh as he leaned in to kiss her again. His fingers unerringly found her wet heat. She whimpered, only to kiss him back even harder.

Then she made small mewling sounds, breaking the kiss to gasp out, "Oh my god, Loki!" before a rush of wetness coated his fingers.

That was the second time she'd called him a god. He wasn't sure what he liked more – the way she cried out his name, or those sweet sounds she made just before she peaked. Did it matter? He wanted more of all of it.

When her third orgasm made her flop down on the bed, unable to sit upright any more, Loki could no longer resist – he had to taste her, to see if she truly was as sweet as she felt.

He lifted her legs over his shoulders, leaning in to inhale her musky scent. He swept his tongue over that small bundle of nerves he knew drove her wild, eliciting another whimper. Faster, harder.

More whimpers as she lifted her hips off the bed, as if inviting him deeper.

Rougher, harder, his hands fastening around her waist as she writhed beneath him.

Whimpering became mewling, until…

"Oh, god, Loki!"

He lapped at her sweetness, then surrendered to temptation and drove his tongue in deep. Oh, by all the gods, he'd never tasted anything so sweet.

Magic lengthened his tongue, letting him stroke places deep inside her that made her shiver and whimper, until she cried out his name again and again.

He was drunk on her pleasure, on her essence. He'd gladly spend all night, every night, wringing those sweet sounds from her lips as her body thrummed with the pleasure only he could give her.

He barely noticed as his trousers became uncomfortably, then impossibly tight. He didn't care. It was Jorunn's pleasure that consumed him. One more orgasm, then another, just to hear her call him a god once more…

"Please, Loki," she whimpered.

"You are insatiable," he said, replacing his tongue with his fingers. Fingers he made longer, thicker, the better to pleasure her, as he leaned over to kiss her.

"I want you to fuck me," she said, before whimpering became mewling.

He pumped his fingers inside her, circling that bundle of nerves with a firm thumb.

"I want more…more!" she cried. "God, Loki, I need your cock!"

He could not refuse her. Off came his trousers and boots, until he was as naked as she was. Then he grabbed her arms and dragged her up the bed, until her head hit the pillow.

Oh, he wanted her. More than anything. He could still feel her wet heat clenching around his fingers – how much better would it be to feel her wrapped around his cock?

But if there were no witches here, there

were no potions to prevent pregnancy, like the women of his time took.

She seemed to read his mind, flapping a hand off the side of the bed. "Condoms in my bag. The side pocket."

He reached into the pouch she pointed at, only to pull out what appeared to be a fake phallus in a most improbable shade of green. Instead of one head, it had several, all stacked up, creating ridges all along its length, with a sort of thumb stuck to one side. He touched one of the small circles on its side, and the thing began to hum and lengthen in his hand.

Jorunn's face flushed. "Oh, that's not…you didn't need to see…" She grabbed the device and flicked the circle, so it lay inert in her hand. Then she stuffed it back into the pouch, and pulled out several small, crinkling squares instead.

Loki couldn't help thinking about the fake phallus. What she'd look like as she thrust it between her thighs. Would she whimper and mewl for it like she did for him? What if he were to…

All other thoughts flew out of his head as her warm fingers stroked down his shaft, unrolling a sort of thin sheath along his length. Such a thing would trap his seed, without stopping sensation. Even the stroke of her fingers was almost more than he could take. If he didn't get inside her soon, he was not going to last long enough…

Her eyes were dark with desire as she lay back, spreading her legs wide. "Fuck me, Loki. Please."

EIGHTEEN

The god of mischief was also the god of orgasms – who'd have guessed? His tongue, his hands…after about the third orgasm, she was certain she wouldn't be able to walk without her legs shaking, but who needed to walk when she never wanted to leave her bed, as long as he was in it? And she hadn't even touched his cock…

As if he'd read her mind, he'd freed it, but

now he seemed to hesitate, like he was looking for…

"Condoms. In my bag. The side pocket," she managed to say.

Of course, the god of mischief found her vibrator first.

What would he say if she told him every time she used it from now on, she'd be imagining it was him? Or him using it on her. She couldn't put it away fast enough.

She needed to feel his cock inside her. Because after all those orgasms, her clit was now so sensitive even the slightest breath across it made her whimper. The next time she came, she wanted it to be with him.

A god. An actual Norse god.

"Fuck me, Loki. Please." Did it sound like she was begging? Because she totally was.

He settled between her thighs, the heat of his head just touching her clit.

He was killing her, making her wait like this. "Please!"

He glided into her, in one super-slow thrust.

"More, please!"

A second thrust, just as slow as the first. Then a third.

"More. Please, Loki, I need more!"

He was already balls deep inside her, and yet…it felt like he was growing longer, and thicker, stretching her more than any man had before.

Another thrust, agonising slow so she could feel every…were those ridges? All the way along his length, rubbing against all the right spots on every thrust…

Jorunn let out a moan, followed by another.

She could feel her orgasm building, thrust by tortuously slow thrust. She wanted to tell him, to ask if he was close, but no words would come out. Just whimpers and moans at the indescribable sensations making her whole body sing, increasing with every stroke. All the while, his eyes on her, drinking in her pleasure as surely as he was feeding it to her.

Oh god oh god she was going to come and she wasn't sure she could take it. Better than his fingers, better than his tongue, his cock was driving her to heights she hadn't even been able to imagine and…

Deep inside her, she felt a bass vibration. Exactly like the vibrator, except…harder. Stronger. Hotter. As those mischievous eyes seared her very soul…his fucking enormous ridged cock pulsed all the way to her core. Then he grinned, tilting her hips just a little so his cock hummed against her clit…

"Oh god, Lokiiiiiiiiiiiiii!" she screamed.

NINETEEN

Jorunn was so exquisitely tight around his cock, that wet heat caressing him with every stroke, Loki lost all reason. And then when she screamed his name…

The music in the halls of Valhalla could not sound half as good.

Probably a good thing he'd made sure the warm bubble enclosing her tent also kept the sound in, for he had no intention of only making her scream once. Over and over he brought her to the peak of pleasure, barely holding on to his own control as she clenched down hard enough on his cock to crush him, or milk him of enough seed to sire an army.

"Oh god, Loki…"

"Oh my god, Loki…"

"God, Loki…"

He would never tire of the sound of her screaming his name, but her voice was growing hoarse, and her inner walls longer squeezed him quite as hard now. It was nearly dawn, and he was supposed to…supposed to…

He could resist her no longer. When her mewling paused long enough for her to suck in a desperate breath, which he knew she was about to expel in one more joyful scream, he let out an answering roar, pouring his own pleasure into her as she drank his.

Afterwards, she lay panting on the bed, her eyes closed with exhaustion, but the sweetest smile graced her lips.

This had been the best night of his life, Loki

decided, as he reluctantly moved away from her to clean himself up and dispose of the sheath. He had precious little time before dawn, and he still had to find that brooch.

But he could not bring himself to regret a single moment spent in Jorunn's bed. Sure, he'd been seducing her in order to get the brooch, but that didn't mean he couldn't enjoy it. Or perhaps come back another night to do it again…

She was sleeping now, utterly spent. He should use this time to find it, so he could spirit it away without her ever knowing he'd taken it, so she'd be willing to take him to her bed again…

TWENTY

Was it possible to get addicted to orgasms? Or maybe just sex. Or Loki. None of the Norse legends or Marvel movies had ever mentioned he had a cock like an enormous human vibrator. Probably because the guys who'd written those legends hadn't slept with him…

Dreamily, Jorunn opened her eyes. He'd draped her sleeping bag over her like a blanket, but she was still naked. Good thing whatever spell he'd cast still made the tent warm, or she'd be freezing her tits off around now.

Something toppled, and Loki swore. He'd knocked over the spare folding chair beside the table they used as a laptop desk, and that had tipped over Sibyl's backpack, still filled with the stuff she'd left behind. Stuff she would come back for.

Stuff she would not appreciate Loki rooting through like he was looking for something, which he evidently hadn't found.

"What are you looking for?" Jorunn asked.

He jumped up in surprise. "The brooch you stole. The gold and amber one."

Even in her post coital bliss, Jorunn's mind was still sharp. "Ah, so you didn't wake up from your thousand year sleep just to fuck me. You woke up to find that brooch, and that's why you seduced me." She should have been angry. Or upset. Or…something, at least. Instead, she just felt empty. Of course no Norse god could possibly want someone as damaged as her. Somehow, with his godly powers, he knew she'd been a thief and believed she'd stolen again.

Well, the joke was on him this time. She'd gotten a night of the best sex of her life – sex she would never forget – and he was going to be leaving empty handed.

"While I admit archaeology is a bit of a grey area when it comes to theft – tomb robbing and the like – that brooch was just lying there in the rocks, where someone had evidently dropped it. Like our expedition leader said, all the things we're finding here belong to the world. It's our history."

Loki frowned. 'That cloak pin belonged to Odin's wife, before she was murdered, and he never removed it. Whoever stole it from him must have dropped it, and he will not treat you kindly if you try to keep it from him. But if you give it to me, I can return it to him without him ever knowing you stole it."

Men. Didn't believe you, even when you were telling the truth, when they'd got some stupid idea in their heads. "I don't have it," she said.

She expected him to be disappointed, but his expression only hardened. "If you tell me where it is, I might be willing to share your bed for another night like this one."

Might, not would, she noted. "Yeah, even if I had it, or knew where it was, I'm not trading valuable artefacts for sex. With you, or Saint Nik."

"Who is this saint you speak of?"

Jorunn laughed. "Oh, he's no saint. He's a right dodgy bastard who's trying to blackmail me into having sex with him or he'll lie about me stealing stuff. Which makes me think he's the one stealing things, and if anyone has the brooch, it's him. Now he might be interested in your deal – sex for stealing stuff – but I don't know if he's into men."

Loki stared at her for a long moment, like he was trying to read her soul. "Can you tell me honestly that you truly do not possess Odin's brooch?"

Something tingled across her bare skin

beneath the sleeping bag, like he was touching her with some sort of spell. "Yes. You could fuck me into next week, and while I'd definitely enjoy every minute of it, I still couldn't give you the brooch, because I don't have it. I put it in the box with all the other artefacts we've found – arrowheads, mostly – but when I went back to look for it, it was gone. Stolen, I suspect."

His shoulders sagged. "And what of Thor's hammer?"

"So it really is Thor's hammer? I told Sibyl it was! Oh, wait until she comes back so I can tell her…" She caught sight of Loki's grave expression and sobered. "We had the hammer in the mess tent, melting the ice off it, and Karl packed it away to send to the lab with Sibyl. She'll know where it is, but I warn you, it's probably locked away in a temperature controlled cabinet by now, and seeing as she's likely to want to base her PhD and a whole bunch of research papers on it, she'll never let it go. Not for sex or money or…even you, actually. She's more into Thor than you." She shrugged. "Sorry."

Only…he didn't look upset. A little perked up, in fact. "Then Thor will find it, and when he holds his hammer again, it will surely break the spell over him. This is good. If only we can find the brooch before Odin wakes, everything will be as it should be." He nodded, then walked out of the tent, and vanished.

TWENTY-ONE

All day, Loki remained in the rocks beneath the camp, waiting for the sun to go down. He could hear and see the other scholars remaining close to their tents and each other, so he had no opportunity to slip into the camp to search for the brooch.

He would likely need Jorunn's help to find it, for she knew her people better than him. Which meant he would have to return to her when the sun set, and persuade her to help him.

No easy task, seeing as she already knew he'd seduced her once for that. She wouldn't fall for that again. Which was a pity, because after last night, all he could think about was sharing her bed again and those sweet sounds she made as he pleasured her…

Loki closed his eyes. He had priorities. He needed to kill Erik and the rest of his family. In order to do that, he would need the help of both Thor and Odin. In order to get Thor's help, he would need to break the spell binding Thor to the girl named Sibyl, and reunite Thor with his hammer. Odin's help would be harder to get, especially if he believed Erik's accusations of treachery. Which meant Loki would have to bring the brooch as a gift, as well as information on how they could defeat Erik, for Odin wanted the jarl dead just as much as he did. As did Thor.

Not to mention he had no idea where Odin even was right now.

But he'd find him. He had to.

Could Loki step aside and let Odin or Thor deal Erik's death blow? He'd vowed to kill the man, and his family, and he was fairly sure he'd succeeded in poisoning both of Erik's sons. Only the witch daughter remained, and once she was gone...perhaps he'd be willing to let the other men take their turn at vengeance. As long as Loki could watch while Erik died.

He'd make the girl's death quick. Witch or not, she did not deserve to suffer.

Which still left him without the brooch.

So...Jorunn. He would beg her for her help, and offer her a boon in return. Anything that was within his power to give. As long as she didn't ask him to spare Erik's life...he would agree to anything else she desired.

TWENTY-TWO

If anything, Saint Nik was even more irritable than usual. It seemed a mosquito had gotten into his tent, and tried to drink all his blood, or at least that's the story he told. Jorunn hoped all his itching was actually some sort of embarrassing rash that had spread to the rest of his body that would result in him needing a medical evacuation, but it seemed the universe had decided that after granting her last night's one night stand with Loki, it was now going to ignore any and all wishes she might have, no matter how much better the universe would be for it.

So she bit her tongue as she sorted through the reindeer bones they'd found, identifying which ones showed signs of human activity, and which ones didn't. She'd probably still scan all of them once they got back to the lab, but at least she could prioritise the smaller pile.

She sighed. She knew there were thousands of reindeer in the national park, but all she'd seen were the bones of long dead ones. Was it too much to ask to see just a single live reindeer while she was here?

"Will you stop taking up all the table space with these worthless bones? There have been reindeer here forever. There is nothing special about them, and they should all be tossed in the trash," Nik snapped.

For a moment, she considered emulating John Wick and killing him with the pencil in her hand. Except…she wasn't an assassin, and she'd probably only break her pencil without doing any kind of damage to Nik.

"Fine," she huffed, packing the bones into boxes, before leaving the mess tent entirely.

The sky outside was leaden grey, threatening snow that didn't seem to want to fall. It was only a little after lunchtime, but it was dark enough to make her think it was dusk. Well, that and she hadn't had much sleep last night, what with Loki and his magic cock. Maybe she should just take a nap while she could. Someone would wake her if she was needed.

Ah, but first she should probably put Sibyl's bed back on her side of the tent, before anyone saw the beds pushed together and got the wrong idea.

But as she hoisted the bed across the divide, something heavy flumped to the floor at her feet. Loki had left his cloak. She lifted it to her nose and inhaled. It smelled of smoke and ash and him.

It looked similar to the one Thor had given Sibyl, which made sense, if the garments were around the same age. They might have even been spun and woven by the same person, if it came to that. But while this was rough wool on the outside, the inside was lined with soft fur. Fur that must have come from a great many creatures, for the lining was a patchwork of pieces. She was certain there was a story behind it – she'd have to ask Loki if he came back for it.

Unless he never came back, and he'd left it as a gift…one she'd gladly accept, seeing as the tent was rather cold without his magic at work. So she wrapped herself in the furry cloak, threw her sleeping bag over the top so anyone who came in wouldn't see it and ask questions, and drifted off into a doze.

TWENTY-THREE

She was already asleep when he entered the tent, though the sun had not even set yet. Between the dark clouds blotting out the sun and the snow drifting down from them, Loki knew he was as safe for sunlight as though night had already fallen.

Only to find her asleep, in a camp full of people who were all awake.

Well, none of the others had been engaged

in bed play into the early hours of the morning, so perhaps they did not need sleep as much as she did.

Loki settled on the empty bed, now pushed back against the tent wall, to wait for Jorunn to wake.

She'd wrapped herself in his cloak, he noticed with a mix of surprise and satisfaction. Perhaps she was not as angry at his betrayal as he'd thought.

Or maybe she'd just claimed his cloak out of spite, after the way he'd treated her, which would be fair.

But he couldn't help thinking about how much he'd loved seeing her naked body spread out across his cloak last night, writhing in ecstasy on the soft fur from the prey of a thousand hunts. How much he'd love to give her a thousand orgasms on the cloak of a thousand hunts…or even more.

Almost without thinking, he recast the bubble spell from last night, turning her tent into a warm haven that the noise and chill from outside could not penetrate, while the sounds of their conversation could not be heard outside of the tent's confines. He had no desire to alert the brooch thief that they were hunting for him. Or her, though with only one other woman in the camp besides Jorunn, it seemed more likely their thief was a man.

Her breathing changed, becoming less even and decidedly rapid.

A little like last night, only…

With a muttered oath, she suddenly sat up, peering around the tent as though expecting to find someone hiding there.

Loki had no intention of hiding. He raised a hand in greeting. "Good evening, Jorunn. I hope you slept well."

She stared at him, her eyes wild. "What the fuck are you doing here?"

He definitely had some work to do if he intended to elicit her assistance. "I have been watching you sleep and reminiscing about the delightful night we spent together. I see you have taken a fancy to my cloak. Consider it a gift, in grateful thanks for the pleasure you gave me last night."

He half expected her to toss the cloak aside in disgust, but she only wrapped it more tightly around herself. "Watching a girl sleep is stalkerish and creepy. Then again, maybe it's a god thing. Is that what you and the other Norse gods do all day? Just sit around and watch people, when you're not interfering with the world? I can imagine Thor watching wrestling or rugby day and night, while Frigg would surely spend all her time watching cat videos. I would've thought you'd be more into candid camera sort of stuff, with people playing pranks on one another."

Loki smiled and inclined his head. Even after only a night, she knew him well. "I do indeed enjoy a good prank, but I prefer to be the one playing them, when I do not have more serious matters to attend to." Like now. When Erik was dead, then he could plan some elaborate prank, something that would make even Jorunn laugh.

She blew out a breath. "I knew you hadn't come here to tell me that you'd fallen for me so completely last night that now you want to carry me off to your castle in the sky."

She had such a way with words. He only wished he could, but… "I do not have a castle, let alone one in the sky. I suppose there is Valhalla, but for that, we would both need to be dead, and I would not wish that for you. I, myself, have a considerable number of things I intend to do before I die, and…" He found she was staring at him, that same wry smile on her lips. "I have said something wrong?"

Slowly, she shook her head. "So if you did have a castle in the sky, you would want to take me there?"

"A castle, a cottage, a longhouse…if I had a home to take you to, where you might have the blazing fire and bigger bed you asked for last night, I would, Jorunn. By all the gods, I would take you to bed for a week, or a whole month's honeymoon, if you'd let me. If I had not sworn oaths that I dare not break…if my life were my own…"

"So why are you here, then?"

Loki took a deep breath. "I have come to beg for your help."

"Go on."

He swallowed. "Do you believe in magic?"

"A week ago, I probably would have said no. But now I've met you and Thor and then there was last night…I'm a scientist, Loki. A scholar. I believe in what I can perceive with my senses, and I know you're really here. I didn't imagine Thor's hammer. So I would have to say…yes, I believe there is more to this universe than we currently understand, and for lack of a better word, we can call it magic. Fuck knows what else I can call that thing you did last night that turned this tent toasty enough to get naked without freezing our arses off."

It was enough. It would have to be.

Loki opened his mouth and out spilled…everything. Losing his family and his village. Living in Odin's village with Thor's family. His vow for vengeance. The failed raid on Utgard…all the way to waking up here.

Finally, he paused for a breath.

She hadn't interrupted. Through all of it, she'd just listened, sky-blue eyes focussed entirely on him, nodding occasionally, but always looking thoughtful. Like she believed him.

"Will you help me?" he asked.

"Let me get this straight. A thousand years ago, you vowed vengeance on a Viking jarl whose army killed your family, before he destroyed the village that had taken you in, so all the surviving men came with you to kill Erik, only you tried to sneak in early and got caught. His witches tried to get you to turn traitor, even telling Odin you were a traitor, and put a spell on you that put you to sleep until you woke up now, with Thor, and you need my help…" She paused. "Actually, that's the bit I don't understand. What do you need my help with?"

"I need you to help me find Odin's brooch,

so I can bring it back to him, to show him I'm not a traitor, and when we break the spell on Thor, we can kill Erik. And his witches."

Doubt clouded her expression. "You want me to help you kill witches and a Viking warrior?" She shook her head. "Look, I came to Norway to get away from my family, and to maybe see some reindeer and the northern lights, so I can do a bunch of research so that in the end people will call me Doctor and maybe even listen to what I have to say. I didn't come halfway around the world to kill people for a grudge you and the other gods have had for a thousand years. I have come close to killing Nik a few times, but I've never tried to actually do it."

Jorunn, the scholar who was all softness and sweetness? Oh, but she had strength, too, and fierceness. It would truly be a joy to fight at her side, if she chose to fight for him. But not yet. Loki laughed. "Gods, no. I need your help to find Odin's brooch, so he and Thor will help me." He dropped to his knees and clasped her hands in his. "I will do anything you ask, if you will just help me to steal that brooch back from the thief who took it."

Again, she looked thoughtful. "I'm tempted to ask you to take out Nik, but if he's the thief, like I think he is, just catching him in the act will be enough. So…yes, I guess I will help you."

He kissed her. Deep and long and oh so sweet. He didn't want to stop, but he knew he must. "Thank you, Jorunn. What can I offer you in return? Anything. If it is within my power to give it to you, then you shall have it."

Her expression turned wistful. "I don't suppose you know where we might find a herd of reindeer…"

"I will find one for you," Loki promised. He led her outside into the snow, then transformed into a wolf and headed toward the pass, sniffing the air.

TWENTY-FOUR

"This is insane. We should stay in camp, with the others, where it's safe," Jorunn said. "You said you wanted my help searching for a brooch, not seeking hypothermia in the snow."

Loki just shook himself, whined at her, and walked on.

Insanity seemed to be the theme of the night. The story he'd told her about all the things that had brought him here had sounded crazy, and yet he hadn't sounded like he was lying. Sure, it hadn't sounded anything like the Norse mythology she'd heard, but stories could get seriously twisted over the centuries. Only now she was following a divine wolf man who wanted to kill people in revenge for something they'd done over a thousand years ago, and twisted didn't begin to cover half of it.

Though it definitely did describe the path they were following…

If she fell into a crevasse or started an avalanche, she was going to kill Loki.

But even with the fog or cloud or whatever it was obscuring her vision, Loki never moved far enough ahead to be out of sight. Better yet, the path he was leading her along seemed like a much easier way up the mountain than the one they'd taken with Jakop and the packhorses to get here. Almost like he knew what he was doing.

The dude had shapeshifted into a dog. Or maybe a wolf. She wasn't actually sure of the difference – her comparative biology was all about reindeer and other prey animals. The only times she cared about wolves and the like was what marks their teeth made when they brought down prey, so she knew it hadn't been human hunters.

Now, however…she was the one most likely to be eaten by wolves. Or one wolf. Was that why Loki had lured her up here? So he could eat her? She hadn't heard anything linking Loki to cannibalism in any of the legends, but she hadn't heard of him being able to shift into a wolf, either, so nothing would surprise her.

She snorted. Maybe that's where Alligator Loki had come from in the Marvel television series. He'd shifted and gotten stuck. She'd have to ask him when they got back if he could turn into an alligator. If they got back and she didn't die by falling into a crevasse or off a cliff or get attacked by a pack of wolves. Or worse. Weren't there bears up here?

Loki led the way up to the edge of a cliff,

and then sat, for all the world like an obedient dog who wanted a treat. Or one of her fingers, more like.

He stared at her expectantly.

"Fine," she huffed, and climbed up beside him. Only to find she couldn't breathe at what she saw.

The peak behind her parted the clouds, so she could see clear to the sea. And what she could see…was a wonder.

A herd of reindeer milled about on the snow, chomping on something that the light snowfall hadn't managed to cover yet.

Finally. All her life, she'd wanted to see reindeer, and there had to be twenty or thirty of them, right in front of her.

Then she looked up, and forgot all about the reindeer.

"Is that the aurora? The northern lights?" she asked, marvelling at the coruscating colours as they reflected off snow, clouds and the distant sea. "I thought you could only see those in winter, not summer. I wish I'd brought my camera. This is freaking amazing." She dropped to her knees beside Loki, and wrapped her arms around him. "Thank you."

He cuddled into her, making a sound that was almost like a rumbling purr. Not something that usually came out of a dog, but then he wasn't really a dog, was he?

She wasn't sure how long they sat there, just watching the light show, until the fog started to press in, and the light faded.

Loki shoved at her as he rose to his feet. And kept rising, which made no sense.

"What?" she asked, turning to look at him. The wolf was gone, replaced by a sturdy looking pony with shaggy fur. A pony who jerked his head toward his back expectantly. "You expect me to ride you back to camp?"

She wasn't sure how a pony could possibly look smug, but he did, when he nodded.

She had to force herself not to check if he was hung like a horse as she climbed on. She was still aching from last night, so she knew as a human, he was definitely big enough to satisfy her. If only he'd be willing to do it again…

But even with the heat of him between her thighs, it was hard to think about anything else other than not falling off, as the path narrowed to where there was a precipitous drop on either side that the fog had hidden from her before. He trotted off down the mountain, and she dug her hands into his mane and hung on.

If he got her back to camp safely, then she could think about…whatever she was starting to feel for this man. God. Horse. Wolf. Whatever.

The god of mischief, definitely. What else he was…she could worry about that later.

TWENTY-FIVE

Loki shouldn't be enjoying this. He didn't like being a horse. But if it meant having Jorunn on his back, right up close to him, he didn't mind it so much. Besides, he could hardly let her head down the mountain on her own. She might stumble off a cliff and get herself killed. She wasn't made of living stone, the way he was.

Some small creature scurried ahead of him,

running along the edge of the ridge until it sloped down, and hid the creature from sight. A rabbit, maybe? As a horse, the runner meant little to him. Now, if he'd still been in his wolf form, or even an owl, he would have taken off after it, and maybe turned it into a lining for the hood of his cloak, but right now, he just kept plodding along, protecting the drowsing woman he…

Loki stopped. No. He wasn't protecting her. That's what THEY wanted him to do. Erik and his pet witches.

Then again, he was fairly certain Jorunn wasn't one of Erik's people, and definitely wasn't a witch. So if he was protecting her, as his instincts were screaming at him to do, it couldn't possibly be Erik's doing. Just something strange to do with the spell that he hadn't managed to entirely break.

But he would, he promised himself. He would. Thor might want to remain in the spell's thrall forever, like the gormless oaf he was, because fighting and protecting was what he wanted to do anyway. Not to mention the dark sprite who'd enchanted him – someone that delicate needed protecting. Not like Jorunn, who was every bit a shieldmaiden, even if she didn't own an actual shield.

So why was he carrying Jorunn home now? Well…

He'd led her up the mountain, and she'd trusted him, something few people did, so he supposed he was honouring that trust by taking her home safely. Not that she couldn't have walked beside him instead of riding, or even finding her own way, with that curious light she wore on her head lighting the way.

And he wouldn't mind the feel of her body on top of his in other, more intimate circumstances…and without the fur, of course. Or clothes. Definitely without the clothes.

He'd give his life for another night with her like last night…

None of the women in Odin's village had ever trusted him the way Jorunn did, or looked at him that way, either. Once or twice, he'd fancied Thor's sister, Sif, might have, but she'd never actually asked him to take a tumble with her, and he'd never had the courage to ask, and then she'd been gone. Then again, if he had, he'd probably have had to contend with Thor's wrath, which would have outweighed all the pleasure from a night in his sister's bed.

So Sif had never really been an option for him.

And now…

Now he was branded a traitor to his people, and no one but Jorunn believed him trustworthy enough to listen to him. Even Thor thought he'd stolen his hammer. As though he'd want to wield that bulky hunk of metal. Give him a throwing axe or a knife, and a place to hide, and Loki was in his element, but in an open battle, he was the worst kind of warrior. He was a scout for a reason, and he was good at it.

Except when he'd been captured by Erik's men…

Like a rabbit in a trap, as helpless as the

running creature up on the ridge.

Loki sighed. He was a good scout. The best. Except that once.

He'd even confessed his failure to Jorunn, and she hadn't hated him for it. She'd still offered to help him. Which made her stand high above all the women he'd ever known, even if he wasn't already in love with her. She knew him, saw into his heart like no one else.

It wasn't like he'd betrayed Odin and his men on purpose. He hadn't said a word to Erik or his witches, no matter what they threatened him with. Even when he'd thought they'd kill him, still he'd stayed silent.

Death might be preferable to this, though. Because when he saw Odin again, and Odin believed Erik's lies, the look of disappointment on the man's face was more than Loki could take.

But right now, it was just him and Jorunn, approaching the camp. Where there was a tent with a bed and hours before dawn which he knew exactly how he wanted to fill…

TWENTY-SIX

Jorunn wasn't quite sure how it happened. One moment, she'd been drowsing on Loki the pony's back, and the next, he was carrying her in his very human arms into her tent, laying her on her bed and…fuck, he was good. And hot and hard and…divine.

When she woke at dawn, he was gone, but he returned at sunset, and one thing had led to another, and…

By day, she searched through the boxes of artefacts, trying and failing to find an opportunity to sneak into Nik's tent to search it, but with everyone confined to camp by the bad weather, sneaking anywhere was impossible.

By night, Loki fucked her senseless, and then fucked her some more, because the sex was just so amazing she couldn't bear to stop.

Finally, in the pale predawn light, as she watched Loki fasten his pants and pull on his boots, ready to depart, she blurted out, "Why don't I try to do what you did? Pretend to seduce him, drug his drink so he falls asleep, and then search his tent while he's passed out?"

"I did not pretend to seduce you, nor did a drug you," Loki growled.

No. He'd definitely seduced her, and she hadn't even touched a drop of the aquavit since Sibyl left. Loki was addictive, all by himself. "I'm sorry, it's just that I thought…"

"Do you want to seduce this man?" His

expression was thunderous.

Jorunn shuddered. "Fuck, no. I'd rather blow the ice man Karl keeps hoping to find."

"Then we will not discuss this further. We will find a way to search his tent for the stolen brooch, and this bastard will not lay a finger on you." Loki reached out and trailed his own finger up the inside of her thigh, stopping short of plunging it into her core.

They'd spent all night together, and here she was, opening her mouth to beg for more.

"We will find another plan. Perhaps when the weather clears and you all walk down by the lake, to survey the site, as you say, you and I will conduct our search. Yes?" His finger stroked her, lightly, tantalisingly, but her clit was so sensitive after a night of his ministrations, she nearly came again on the spot.

"Yes," she whimpered, as he continued to stroke.

"Your sweetness is mine alone and I will not share you with a common thief. Not for

Odin, or vengeance for a dozen villages, or anything," Loki swore.

She let out a cry as one more burst of ecstasy engulfed her, but when she opened her eyes, he was gone.

TWENTY-SEVEN

Finally, the inevitable happened. Sibyl returned, and sunset found Jorunn sitting in her tent, staring at the stuff on Sibyl's bed. There was no way she and Loki would be able to get up to mischief with Sibyl here. She ached for him already, and she knew she only had moments before he appeared. What was she going to do?

"Thor has agreed to provide a distraction,"

Loki said. "Come, I need you to peek into the feasting hall tent, to see if everyone is there, and if they are, you must come and help me with the search." He tapped his lips. "There's just one small thing. We also need to look for his hammer."

Jorunn rubbed her face, trying to wrap her head around the change of plans. From looking forward to incredible sex to not knowing how to tell him they couldn't to now trying to find Thor's hammer a second time, when it had been a miracle to find it the first time?

Finally, she just shook her head. Miraculous or not, they were doing this.

"Right. Let's find Frigg's brooch and Thor's hammer," Jorunn said.

"But first you must check the feasting hall," Loki insisted.

"Okay."

Jorunn slipped into the mess tent, which was particularly crowded tonight.

"Everybody must drink a toast to our

handfasting!" roared a blonde bloke who could easily have posed as a Hemsworth brother. Until he turned to kiss Sibyl's cheek, and Jorunn had to admit he was better looking than any actor. No wonder Sibyl was blushing.

Wait, hang on…handfasting? Wasn't that a sort of Viking wedding ceremony?

"Are you sure about this?" Lara asked, looking at Sibyl.

"I have never been more certain of anything in my life!" the blonde blustered. He had to be Thor.

Sibyl didn't look so certain, though. She muttered something about getting more mead.

"Don't let them leave!" Loki hissed from outside.

Jorunn pasted a fake grin on her face. "I'll go get the rest. Be right back," she said, slipping back out.

Loki grabbed her arm and pulled her toward the nearest tent. "Which one belongs to the thief?"

Jorunn pointed. "That one. But did you

know Thor was planning on marrying my roommate, who he's only known for a matter of days?"

Loki shrugged. "They both must agree to the handfasting. If she does not wish to have him, she can refuse. Thor is many things, but he would never force a woman against her will. Or is this because I did not agree to a handfasting with you before I bedded you? You were certainly willing, so I did not consider it necessary at the time, but if you wish me to say the words that will make you mine…"

The way he growled that last word sent tremors right through her core. Almost enough to make her agree to this madness.

Jorunn yanked her hand out of Loki's. "I'm not going to marry you! Bad enough that my roommate's insane enough to do it. Like you'll even remember I exist after we find this brooch. You'll vanish, like you do every morning, and I'll never see you again!"

Loki looked hurt. "I promise you, Jorunn,

no matter how long I live, I will never forget a moment spent in your company. We must find the brooch, and Thor's hammer, and Odin, but afterwards…when this is done, if you wish to be handfasted, my pledge is yours. In fact, any other man who touches you, I will find it very difficult not to kill him."

Jorunn closed her eyes. The world had gone mad, and Loki was crazier still. "Loki…"

"I do not need your answer now, sweet shieldmaiden. Right now, I need your help searching for a thief's hoard, and a hammer."

Yes. Searching Nik's tent, while he was stuck in that insane ceremony with everyone else.

Loki did most of the actual searching, while Jorunn opened things or identified items that left Loki perplexed. No hammer, no brooch…they didn't find a single artefact in Nik's tent, even after Jorunn had patted down his pillow and sleeping bag.

Where had he hidden them?

Then she flipped over his bed, and hit

paydirt. A bulging pouch had been taped to the underside, but when she looked inside…

"Just a satphone," she said in disgust, wanting to smash it against the rocks outside out of sheer frustration.

"What do these things do?" Loki asked, poking a button.

Loki and buttons. At least it wasn't a vibrator.

"That's it!" Loki exclaimed. He turned the satphone over. "Now, how do I get it out?"

Jorunn blinked. On the satphone screen was a picture of the brooch, sitting on a record card. Nik had stolen it!

She flipped through the pictures. The brooch, other items of jewellery, heaps of coins…and Thor's hammer, glinting like it was brand new, instead of buried in the ice for a thousand years. She kept scrolling, but that was the end of the artefact pictures. The rest were just waste containers, like the one they transported the toilet waste in. The sort of thing no one noticed or opened or cared about when they were loaded up to take back to civilisation…

"That's how he's doing it," she whispered.

"What?" Loki asked. His eyes darted around the tent, desperately searching for somewhere they hadn't looked yet.

"He's getting the artefacts out by pretending they're waste. Hiding them in the waste containers. Nothing's here because he already shipped them out with the supply run. It's all headed back to the lab." Jorunn stared at the screen. "We need to call the lab, or send someone after Jakop and the packhorses…"

"Thor will go. Go back into the feasting tent, and tell him you could not find what you were looking for. He will understand, and come find me," Loki said.

Reluctantly, Jorunn pressed the satphone into Loki's hands. "Don't lose that. It's all the proof we have."

She headed back into the mess tent, babbling at Thor and Sibyl that she hadn't been able to find…whatever it was they'd sent her to get.

Thor transformed from beaming bridegroom to god of thunder in an instant. "Don't worry, we'll go find it," he growled, dragging Sibyl after him.

Jorunn wanted to follow, but Lara wrapped an arm around her waist, pressing a cup of something alcoholic into her hand, insisting she drink a toast to the happy couple.

Everyone cheered and drank, while Jorunn muttered something about this being madness, as she drained her cup.

Oh, fuck, that was potent. Unlike the aquavit, though, sweetness coated the burn all the way down the back of her throat.

Maybe she should have one more cup…

TWENTY-EIGHT

Finally, Jorunn managed to get out of the mess tent and back to hers. Loki was standing outside, still holding the satphone.

"Can I have that?" she asked. "If I show that to Karl, it'll be proof that Nik's the thief, not me."

"Sure," he said, handing it over. "I'll wait for you inside, so we can celebrate." He winked and disappeared into her tent.

Weren't Thor and Sibyl in there? Newlyweds, doing…the sort of stuff just married people did?

She waited for a moment, half expecting to see Loki come flying back out, but nothing happened. Actually, it was pretty quiet, like the tent was empty.

She shook herself. She was just delaying the inevitable. She had to go catch Karl before he went to bed, prove her innocence, once and for all, and then she could go to bed, too.

Jorunn stepped inside the mess tent, phone held out in front of her, only to find the tent was empty.

"So you're thief who went through my tent and stole my phone." Nik stepped into the tent behind her, blocking her exit.

"I'm not a thief – you are, and I have proof!" she said, brandishing the phone.

"You mean a phone full of pictures that could belong to anyone? Right now, it looks like it belongs to you, seeing as you stole it," Nik said.

"I did not! I'm going to give it to Karl and…"

"I'll say it's not mine. That it's yours. Who will he believe? The thief, or the colleague he's known for years?"

Jorunn swallowed. No one ever believed her. No one. Except Loki, and he wasn't here.

Nik held out his hand. "Give me the phone."

Jorunn shook her head. "It's all the proof I have, until someone pays a visit to the lab and looks in the waste containers."

"Proof that incriminates you, not me, as long as you're the one holding the phone. Now, if you give the phone to me, things might go easier for you. Especially if you haven't made any calls yet."

Fuck. She should have tried to call someone. Because all he had to do was make a call, and those waste containers would vanish before anyone could reach them.

Now it was too late.

"Karl will be back in a moment. What'll it

be, Aussie girl? Do you want to be deported as a thief, stripped of your medal, and never work in academia again? Or give me back my phone, keep your mouth shut, and come to my tent tonight to compensate me for the mess you've made?"

Fuck fuck fuck. If they'd found even one artefact. One stolen thing…where had he hidden them all?

Without any proof, it was her word against his, and she knew who Karl believed.

Fuck.

Wordlessly, she handed over the phone.

Just a moment before Karl walked in.

"Nik, Jorunn. I hope you didn't drink too much tonight. The weather report's all clear for tomorrow, so we can walk the site again, and see if the storm uncovered anything new!" Karl was just about dancing at the news.

She glanced at Nik. His hands were empty – no sign of the phone at all. He must have shoved it into his pocket or something.

Jorunn forced out a smile. "I'd better go to

bed. I'll need all the sleep I can get if we're surveying again tomorrow." She hurried out before Nik could follow her.

She'd rather eat pickled herring for eternity than go to Nik's tent tonight, or any night. He could go fuck himself, for all she cared.

She had to find another way to prove her innocence…and his guilt. Damn it, there had to be a way. If only she could think of one…

TWENTY-NINE

Much later that night, as Jorunn lay sated in Loki's arms, she told him what had happened. "I didn't know what else to do," she lamented.

He tweaked her nipple. "That's because you aren't a trickster, like I am. I would have accepted his offer."

She reared up. "You told me you'd kill anyone else who touched me, that you didn't want me to pretend to seduce him!"

"Oh, if he lays one finger on you, I will kill him. Do not doubt that. But you could never pretend to seduce him, or anyone. Desire lights your eyes like the sun in the darkness. For a man you do not like, your expression would be lifeless. Any fool would know you were only pretending."

She wasn't sure Nik cared about that. It wouldn't matter to him whether she wanted him or not – this was about power and control and his pleasure alone. Fucking arsehole. If he ever got into academia, teaching actual students, he was a sexual harassment lawsuit waiting to happen. Then again, some of her tutors back home had been PhD students. Maybe he'd been bullying female students for years already, which would explain how easily he'd turned to trying to manipulate her. How many other girls had he forced into his bed with threats of bad grades or false accusations? Someone had to bring him to justice, the sooner the better.

"Which is why I shall proposition him in

your place," Loki finished.

Jorunn laughed so hard she almost choked. "You? You think Nik would be interested in sleeping with you?"

"He will if he thinks I'm you."

She felt him shift beneath her, sliding out from under her until he stood beside the bed. Just as naked as she was, only…only…

"Fuck," she breathed.

Beside the bed stood her double. Blonde braid half undone, nipples wet and rosy from Loki suckling at them, even her inner thighs still slick from their frenzied lovemaking.

"Have you ever been with a girl, Jorunn?" he…no, she breathed, with a voice that sounded like Loki's but was just a little higher, and with an Aussie accent. "I promise you'll enjoy it."

Jorunn closed her eyes. "Stop. That's just…weird. Watching someone like me make those faces and say those things. Do I really sound like that?"

Loki grinned, and it was definitely his grin,

even if it was on her face. "No. Your kind of seduction is much more straightforward. More… 'Kiss me, Loki,' or 'Fuck me, Loki,' or 'More, please, Loki,' and my favourite, 'Oh my god Loki!'"

Jorunn swallowed. She'd said all those things, several times over, tonight. But the thought of Loki doing any of what they'd done with someone else, man or woman, and looking like her…

She managed a watery smile. "All right, you can pretend to seduce him, but I have one condition."

"Anything."

"If he touches you, he dies."

Loki bowed low. "Your wish is my command, my lady."

A horrible thought occurred to her. "Wait, I didn't mean literally…"

But it was too late. He was already gone.

THIRTY

At sunset the following night, Loki waited until Jorunn had gone to her tent before he made his move. "Nik, can I talk to you outside for a moment, please?" he simpered, beckoning.

He wore the illusion of Jorunn's form, in the same clothing she'd worn today, so as not to make the man suspicious.

Nik stomped out after her. "If this is more pointless accusations, after you did not arrive last night, I will not listen. You have one last chance. Tonight."

Loki wet his lips, letting the little pink tip of Jorunn's tongue tantalise the man the way it did him. Of course, this man would never know the sheer pleasure of Jorunn's tongue as she ran it up the length of his cock…

"I was afraid. I've never…been with a man before," Loki said.

Nik's eyes widened, then got greedy. "I'll be your first?"

"I wanted my first time to be special. On the beach. Can we…go down to the lake? With a blanket? So we're alone?" Loki pleaded. "After everyone's gone to bed, and the moon's up. It'll be more romantic in the moonlight."

Nik snorted. "You silly Aussie girls, with your romance. Tonight, I will teach you everything you need to know about romance." He gave a curt nod. "Meet me by the lake at midnight. If you are late…I'll see that Karl sends you straight back to Australia on the next plane."

Loki ducked his head, trying to appear subservient while actually hiding his smile. This man was so boringly predictable. "Yes, Dr Fridolfsen." He trudged back to Jorunn's tent, waiting until he was inside before he dropped the illusion.

"Did he agree?" she asked.

Loki nodded, peeling off his clothes. "We have until midnight, and I mean to have you in every way possible before then, so that you are sound asleep when I go to seduce that fool of a thief."

Their frenzy of lovemaking was over too soon, and Loki did not want to leave her for the chilly night air, but he could not let her tormentor get away with his crimes, either. By the time the sun rose, he swore, the man would never bother Jorunn again.

Loki stepped out of her tent, clothed in the illusion of a gown he'd found in the bottom of her bag. Thin silk that hid little of what was underneath, even if it reached his ankles. He'd added a coat and a pair of fur-lined boots for warmth, which the real Jorunn would need, though he did not.

He arrived at the lake first, as he'd planned, and laid the illusion of a blanket on a particularly deep patch of ice, which was flatter than the surrounding rocks.

Offering a silent apology to Jorunn, he cast a magic bubble on the air above the blanket, invisible but warm. This wouldn't work unless he could get the man to take his clothes off.

A quarter hour after midnight, the man finally appeared, swaggering down the slope as though he'd stuffed a feather pillow down his pants where his balls should be.

He stopped at the edge of the blanket. No greeting, just staring. "I want you to get naked," he grunted.

"Can I see you first?" Loki asked timorously. He even managed to make his voice tremble.

The brute shrugged out of his jacket, and set it aside. "Your turn."

Loki removed the illusion of a coat, placing

it on the blanket beside him. The sheer silk gown beneath fluttered in a non-existent breeze, plastering it against Jorunn's illusory curves. Loki even poked pretend nipples through it.

Nik let out a grunt of approval, then dropped to the ground to remove first his boots, then his pants, until he sat on the edge of the blanket in just a tunic, within arm's reach of Loki. "Now you."

He'd left her feet bare within the boots, but he hadn't bothered with stockings or hose beneath the gown, and he didn't intend to change the illusion now.

It was Nik's turn to remove his tunic, so Loki just sat there and waited, but the man didn't move. Instead, he said, "Get on your hands and knees."

Glad he was still wearing his boots and trousers beneath the illusion, Loki did as he was bid. He heard the man drop heavily to his knees behind him, before he grasped the gown with both hands and tore it away.

Loki fought to hold the illusion as the man

tossed the ripped gown onto the rocks. He prayed Jorunn would forgive him for allowing this brute to see her naked form, even if it was only an illusion. Then the man's hands came down on his hips and…

Loki shifted, dropping the illusion entirely.

Before he clocked the man with his antlers, sending him sprawling face first on the ice. He waited to see if Nik would get up, but the man stayed down.

Good.

Then Loki began to rub the man liberally with reindeer musk, fresh from the glands of the female reindeer he'd transformed into. One in full oestrus, of course. Occasionally, he stopped to let out a mating call, grinning when he got a response from a male not far away.

Finally, Loki ran out of musk, but it didn't matter. He didn't need it any more. He let out a reedy bellow, like a young male reindeer who couldn't believe his luck, right in the man's ear.

The stunned man woke with a start.

Just as the herd arrived.

THIRTY-ONE

Did Loki seriously expect her to sleep while he went off to seduce Nik into somehow revealing his guilt? It'd been a bad plan when she suggested it, and something told her it would be even worse with Loki involved, so as soon as the sound of his footsteps had faded, she got dressed in her fuck-it's-cold-but-I-need-to-go-outside-anyway gear, and headed out after him.

Nik's tent was cold, dark and empty – where

were they?

She headed up to the ridgeline that sheltered the camp from the worst of the wind. Karl liked to point out the day's survey sites from here, because in daylight, you could see clear down to the lake.

In the moonlight, she could see the shimmering surface of the lake, but everything in between was in shadow. Except for something pale, moving down near the water...

Jorunn squinted, but she couldn't quite make it out.

"I thought you'd appreciate the rutting reindeer. They're quite a sight, aren't they?" Loki asked. He was perched on top of a rock cairn, swinging his legs as he watched whatever was going on down by the lake.

"Where's Nik?" she blurted out.

Loki's teeth flashed white in the moonlight as he grinned. "Under that reindeer. Oh, wait, no, it's finished with him. Now another one's having a go."

Jorunn stared at him. "You mean he's being trampled by a herd of reindeer? We can't just leave him there – they'll crush him and kill him! We have to save him!"

"What happened to touch me and die? I distinctly remember promising…"

"Loki! You can't just kill people!"

"Oh, I think he'll survive. He might wish he was dead, after the whole herd's had him…"

"Loki! You have to help him! I know he's an arsehole, but we need to find out where he's been stashing the stolen stuff."

Loki was still laughing, until he let out a long-suffering sigh. "Do you truly want me to save him from the randy reindeer?"

Reindeer had antlers for a reason – and they were vicious during mating season. Jorunn might not have seen many of them, but she did know that.

"Yes! They could do some serious damage. The antlers, those hooves…"

"Mm, those, too. I suppose I could chase the reindeer away, but they'll only come back.

Well, unless I do something to really frighten them…"

Loki jumped down from the cairn. "Right, my lovely scholar. Tell me if you know what this animal is…"

He dropped to a crouch, then transformed into something that looked like a small bear.

"A bear?"

He shook his head.

"A badger?"

Another headshake.

Jorunn racked her brain for what other species she'd seen listed for the national park. She knew the deer best, and she'd been warned about all the bigger predators. Bears, wolves, lynxes and…

"Wait – is that a wolverine?"

A nod, before he bounded off down the slope.

Faintly, Jorunn heard the sound of running water, followed by an unearthly scream. Then another.

Loki came bounding back up the slope,

shifting from beast to man mid-stride. "You are as wise as you are beautiful, Jorunn. You actually made me think of something worse than being raped to death by randy reindeer."

"What?" Jorunn wasn't sure she wanted to know. He couldn't have just said that, could he?

Loki looked smug. "Having your private parts frozen to a glacier, and being peed on by a territorial wolverine. Nothing will go near him now."

Down by the lake, Nik let out another horrible scream.

Karl and Lara came running up, followed by the others.

"What is it?" Lara asked, peering out into the darkness.

"I think it's Nik. He might be injured," Jorunn said. Loki, of course, had vanished.

"Andreas, get the big torches out of the emergency kit. We'll all go down there together, to be safe," Karl said.

Each armed with a torch, they marched in a

line, just like they did for survey work during the day.

The screams had faded to agonised moans, which meant Nik was still alive, but Jorunn wasn't sure for how long. It sounded bad.

Fredrik spotted him first. "It's Dr Fridolfson!" he shouted, rushing forward to help him up.

"Noooo!" Nik screamed as he threw himself back down on the ground, nearly taking Fredrik down with him. "I'm stuck to the ice!"

Lara was the first to respond. "Back to the mess tent, bring all the warm water you can carry. I'll get to work heating some more."

Karl cautiously approached Nik. "Are you all right? What happened?"

"Slipped. On the ice. Woke up stuck," Nik mumbled.

Jorunn edged closer, not wanting to see but knowing she had to know what Loki had done. Until…

"Oh god, what's that stench?" she yelped.

Karl looked grim. "Wolverine. I've heard people say skunks smell bad, but they're nothing compared to being sprayed by a wolverine. Takes days to wear off, too." He jerked his head up the hill, toward the camp. "You go help Lara and the others. Fredrik and I will stay with him. Fredrik will have to get used to the smell, because he's already got it on him."

Fredrik started swearing.

Jorunn hotfooted it up the hill.

A couple of hours and countless pots of water later, a piece of ice gave way, taking a big patch of Nik's skin with it. With one final scream, he passed out.

It took all four men to roll him onto a stretcher, carefully covered with plastic, before carrying him up the hill.

Jorunn found herself standing alone by the blood streaked ice patch, unable to take her eyes away from it. This was her fault. A man was badly injured because of her.

"Ahh, just a bit of skin. I was hoping the ice

would rip his whole cock off, maybe his testicles, too. Pity," Loki said, appearing at his shoulder.

"Loki! That's a horrible thing to say!"

He shrugged. "He wanted to rape you. Tried to rape me. I'd say he got what he deserved. Meanwhile, you might want to get your colleagues to take a look at his pockets. That satphone thing's in there, along with a whole bag of coins and jewels in a secret pouch in the lining of his coat. Maybe I should thank Erik for it when I see him, for in the end, it was the price of a true traitor. Pretty incriminating, if you ask me."

She wasn't as nice as Sibyl, and while she'd often considered pushing Nik off a glacier, she'd never thought about sticking him to one. Maybe Loki was right, and it did serve him right. She didn't want to say so, though. So, "Thank you," was all she said.

A crack, like a gunshot, came from the ice, then another. Now the ice was floating, on what appeared to be its own tiny lake.

Loki grabbed a stick and flipped one of the icebergs onto the rocks, followed by two more. They both peered into the pool and found a face staring back at them. Or it would have been, if the man's eyes were open.

"Fuck," Jorunn swore, followed by, "Karl! You gotta come and see this!"

"Odin," Loki breathed. "We've found Odin."

ABOUT THE AUTHOR

Demelza Carlton has always loved the ocean, but on her first snorkelling trip she found she was afraid of fish.

She has since swum with sea lions, sharks and sea cucumbers and stood on spray drenched cliffs over a seething sea as a seven-metre cyclonic swell surged in, shattering a shipwreck below.

Demelza now lives in Perth, Western Australia, the shark attack capital of the world.

The *Ocean's Gift* series was her first foray into fiction, followed by her suspense thriller *Nightmares* trilogy. She swears the *Mel Goes to Hell* series ambushed her on a crowded train and wouldn't leave her alone.

Want to know more? You can follow Demelza on Facebook, Twitter, YouTube or her website, Demelza Carlton's Place at:

www.demelzacarlton.com

Books by Demelza Carlton

Siren of Secrets series

Ocean's Secret (#1)

Ocean's Gift (#2)

Ocean's Infiltrator (#3)

Siren of War series

Ocean's Justice (#1)

Ocean's Widow (#2)

Ocean's Bride (#3)

Ocean's Rise (#4)

Ocean's War (#5)

How To Catch Crabs

Nightmares Trilogy

Nightmares of Caitlin Lockyer (#1)

Necessary Evil of Nathan Miller (#2)

Afterlife of Alana Miller (#3)

Mel Goes to Hell series

The Devil's Work (#1)

See You in Hell (#2)

Mel Goes to Hell (#3)

To Hell and Back (#4)

The Holiday From Hell (#5)

All Hell Breaks Loose (#6)

The Devil Goes to Heaven (#7)

Romance Island Resort series

Maid for the Rock Star (#1)
The Rock Star's Email Order Bride (#2)
The Rock Star's Virginity (#3)
The Rock Star and the Billionaire (#4)
The Rock Star Wants A Wife (#5)
The Rock Star's Wedding (#6)
Maid for the South Pole (#7)

Romance a Medieval Fairytale series

Enchant: Beauty and the Beast Retold
Dance: Cinderella Retold
Fly: Goose Girl Retold
Revel: Twelve Dancing Princesses Retold
Silence: Little Mermaid Retold
Awaken: Sleeping Beauty Retold
Embellish: Brave Little Tailor Retold
Appease: Princess and the Pea Retold
Blow: Three Little Pigs Retold
Return: Hansel and Gretel Retold
Wish: Aladdin Retold
Melt: Snow Queen Retold
Spin: Rumpelstiltskin Retold
Kiss: Frog Prince Retold
Reflect: Snow White Retold
Roar: Goldilocks Retold
Cobble: Elves and the Shoemaker Retold
Float: Enchanted Horse Retold
Steal: Forty Thieves Retold
Call: Pied Piper Retold

Feather: Swan Maidens Retold
Curse: Rose Red Retold
Cross: Three Billy Goats Gruff Retold
Weave: Rapunzel Retold
Claim: Puss in Boots Retold

Colony Universe

Cowboys and Aliens
Ghost
Vulcan
Cupid
Valentine
Prometheus
Halcyon
Poseidon
Apollo

Heart of Stone series

Broken Chains
Broken Bonds
Broken Dreams

Heart of Steel series

Stone Guardian
Stone Champion
Stone Sentinel
Stone Shadow

www.ingramcontent.com/pod-product-compliance
Lightning Source LLC
Chambersburg PA
CBHW070638170726

48291CB00003B/1056